Ducking his head, he pressed his cheek to hers and whispered in her ear.

"Tell me, baby."

"It's been a tough year."

Against her temple, she felt the prickle of his brow as it contracted, and she could understand his confusion. Maybe he thought she was referring to her broken relationship with Paul, which was a natural conclusion. The wrong one, but still natural. Tony had only ever known about the tip of her iceberg of secrets.

She couldn't bear the thought of telling him about the rest.

"I understand," he murmured. "I know about tough years."

"I'm strong. I can handle almost anything."

"I know you can."

"The one thing I can't handle," she said, raising her head so she could look him in the eye, even though she was about one second from bawling like a baby, "is having you and then losing you."

A glimmer of something—relief? Hope?—flashed across his face. "You're not going to lose me."

That did it. The first tear fell, splashing down her face. "It's inevitable."

His brow furrowed into a vague frown, but he chose not to pursue it now, which was, she knew, a temporary reprieve at best.

Instead, he lowered his head and, taking all the time in the world, covered her mouth with his.

Books by Ann Christopher

Kimani Romance

Just About Sex
Sweeter Than Revenge
Tender Secrets
Road to Seduction
Campaign for Seduction
Redemption's Kiss
Seduced on the Red Carpet
Redemption's Touch
The Surgeon's Secret Baby
Sinful Seduction
Sinful Temptation

ANN CHRISTOPHER

is a full-time chauffeur for her two overscheduled children. She is also a wife, former lawyer and decent cook. In between trips to various sporting practices and games, Target, and the grocery store, she likes to write the occasional romance novel. She lives in Cincinnati and spends her time with her family, which includes two spoiled rescue cats, Sadie and Savannah; and two rescue hounds, Sheldon and Dexter. As always, Ann is hard at work on her next book, and hopes that—if you haven't already—you'll pick up the first book in her Twins of Sin series, Sandro's story, *Sinful Seduction*, which is still available.

If you'd like to recommend a great book, share a recipe for homemade cake of any kind, or suggest a tip for getting your children to do what you say the *first* time you say it, Ann would love to hear from you through her website, www.AnnChristopher.com.

Sinful
temptation

ANN CHRISTOPHER

KIMANI™
ROMANCE

To Richard

KIMANI PRESS™

ISBN-13: 978-0-373-86249-8

Recycling programs
for this product may
not exist in your area.

SINFUL TEMPTATION

Copyright © 2012 by Sally Young Moore

www.kimanipress.com

Printed in U.S.A.

Dear Reader,

Stateside again after his escape from captivity in Afghanistan, Tony Davies does his best to embrace civilian life, which isn't easy. The war haunts him, and there are things he cannot forget. Like the woman who wrote to him while he was overseas, her poignant letters and the passion he'd begun to feel for her. He'd even nursed the secret hope that they had a future together— until her communication suddenly stopped, leaving him with only unanswered questions and a terrible silence.

Painter Talia Adams is also haunted by her past, and the last thing she expects is to find Tony Davies alive and on her doorstep, demanding explanations she doesn't want to give.

What will she do?

She'd better come to terms with her demons, and fast, because she's about to run headlong into one unavoidable truth: Tony didn't survive all those terrible months as a POW only to return home and lose the woman he's come to love....

Happy reading!

Ann

To the men and women serving in the Armed Forces:

Thank you.

Prologue

Two years ago

August 16
Dear Antonios—

I'm so glad we had the chance to meet at my studio before you went overseas! You do remember me, right? I know it's been a little while. I was the one with the winning smile and all the silver bracelets that you so kindly made fun of.

Ringing a bell? Yes? No? You were there to pick up your nephew Nikolas from my art class in the West Village.

Anyway, I have a confession to make: this whole idea of communicating without email is overwhelming me. I understand that while you're stationed in Afghanistan you'll be in some areas where the internet is unavailable, but, really, it seems very rude of the locals not to provide the best possible accommodations for you. Has anyone explained to them the need for additional towers and the like? Maybe if you point out how important it is…?

In the meantime, I've found an answer to this dilemma. After much research, I've discovered that there is another way to pass along written ideas. It's called writing a letter, and it involves pen and paper. No, really! But it's not a perfect solution. For one thing, have you seen my hand-writing? For another, who will spell-check? My speling and proofreeding arnt what they shood ought to be pritty bad.

Clearly, this whole exercise is fraught with peril, and not for the faint of heart, but I do think I'm up to the challenge.

So…

How are you? You're staying safe, right? Please tell me you're staying safe. And if you see any bad guys with guns and bombs coming, please RUN! They probably don't tell you that during army training, but you should RUN whenever possible. Don't stay and fight. That's just crazy.

Oh, and I wanted to send you a care package with gum, sunscreen and hard candy in it, but my online research (because we have the appropriate number of towers here in New York!) tells me that soldiers get too much gum, sunscreen and hard candy.

Are there any treats you miss from home that I can send you?

Well, that's it for now. Please write me back, unless you're too busy RUNNING, in which case you're excused from writing me back, but only until you're safe again.

Your new pen pal,

Talia

P.S. I promised myself that if I ever wrote to a soldier, I'd tell him this: you are brave and strong, and I'm in awe of you. Thank you for your service.

August 30

Talia—

How could I forget you?

Thank you for writing the "letter."

And thanks for the P.S. Especially the P.S. I don't always feel brave or strong, but I'm trying.

Anyway…

I, too, was unaware that there were such things as "letters" before I came over here, but I really like them, especially when they come from you. Oh, and I did mention your concern about towers to the local tribal leader, but he didn't seem that receptive. Pardon the pun. He blathered something about needing food and shelter for his villagers, before he tried to shoot my head off.

Oh, and that reminds me. I wanted to RUN, but it turns out that soldiers are expected to FIGHT BACK and PROTECT PEOPLE. Who knew? So I will try that for a while and see how it goes.

I miss lots of treats from home. Can you fold up a hot pizza slice from John's Pizzeria and send it along? Or a hot shower? If either of those turn out to be too tricky and won't fit into one of those prepaid postal boxes, I'd love something spicy or salty.

In your next "letter," please tell me about your painting and your students. In my next life, if I'm lucky enough to have one, I'll probably be involved in running the family's auction house. My major at West Point was Art, Philosophy and Literature, so I know just enough about art to be dangerous.

Until next time,

Tony

P.S. That reminds me— If you call me by my crazy-ass full name again, you will have to RUN. It's <u>Tony</u>.

September 14

Dear TONY—

I have sent the hot shower and John's pizza along via FedEx. If you experience any delays in receiving them, please let me know. I did keep the tracking numbers.

Meanwhile, I'm enclosing a pound of wasabi-coated peanuts. They were so spicy that when I tried them, I had to spit them out, soak my tongue in ice water and then proceed to the E.R. for treatment, followed by several rounds of physical therapy. So I figure they're perfect for you!

I know who you are, of course. One of the sons of Davies & Sons. Big auction house. Art.

Antiques. Antiquities. Jewelry. But here's what I don't get—what're you doing in the army? Where'd your father go wrong with you???

What should I tell you about my paintings? I work with oils and acrylics to create abstract representations of nature, emotions and anything else that sparks my imagination. Translation: I paint giant slashes and squiggles in bright colors. Oh, and smudges. Lots of smudges. And I also use my studio to teach painting to kids because, let's face it, most of them understand squiggles.

Exciting, eh? Aren't you glad you asked?

But my reputation is growing and I am selling a lot of portraits these days, which is my bread-and-butter work. After my first solo show about three years ago, I turned a corner and my commissions have really taken off, which is good, since I like to eat and want to travel. Life's short and there's lots to see and experience, you know? So I charge rich people a lot to paint them with their favorite polo ponies and the like, and guess what? They pay it!!! See? Win-win for everyone!

Okay. Your turn. Tell me something about you. What about the wedding plans? How're they coming?

Oh, and today I read an article about service dogs in Afghanistan. Do you have any?

Gotta go—Paul, my sister and my girlfriends are luring me to a new club in the Meatpacking District tonight, where they're throwing me a surprise party for my thirtieth birthday. So I need to work on my astonishment. How's this:

Oh, my God!

Or this:

SHRIEK I don't believe it!!

Or this:

SOBBING I love you guys!!!

Take care and stay safe—

Talia

October 1

Dear Talia—

Thanks for the wasabi peanuts! I ate half of one last night and am still sweating. Awesome! I did have to beat off most of my men, though. Those vultures thought I would share.

Wow. You totally had me fooled on the surprise party thing. Nice job. Which option did you finally go with? The sobbing? How was the party?

You asked about how I wound up in the army. That actually is tied to the auction house. When I was about ten, we conducted the auction of a collection of military memorabilia from the Napoleonic Wars, which was a refreshing change from paintings, jewelry and Tiffany lamps, let me tell you. This led to an obsession with Napoleon... Alexander the Great... Patton... If you can think of a great general, I've read about him. This led me and my brother to West Point, and the rest is history.

But I will get back to the auction house one day. It's in my blood.

What else did you ask about?

Oh, yeah—we do have a service dog—her name is Chesley, and she's a mine-sniffing border collie mix. She's supposed to sleep with her handler, but she's not the faithful type. I've woken up to find her snuggled up to me on more than one memorable occasion. She also enjoyed the wasabi peanuts, so that tells you how cool she is. She's saved our hides many times.

Wedding update? Here it is: there's not going to be one. Skylar dumped my ass before I shipped out. Turns out she doesn't "love me like she should." That's what she says, anyway. So I guess it's good she didn't marry me, eh?

I'm not sure how I feel about the whole thing at the moment, to tell you the truth. Angry? Relieved? Hurt?

What about you and Paul? Any wedding bells and 2.5 kids in your future? If so, tell Paul he's a lucky guy.

Gotta go—lights out—

Tony

October 20
Dear Tony—
SKYLAR SUCKS!!!!!!!!!!!
That is all.
Love, Talia

P.S. I enclosed some Indian snack mix that is even hotter than the wasabi peanuts. Eat with caution! Oh, and some candy, since Halloween is coming up. Hope you like Skittles!

P.P.S. Paul is, of course, lucky, because, let's face it, I'm a fabulous woman. But I'm not sure that I'm ready to settle down or that he's THE ONE, whatever that means. Although he does throw a great surprise party with plenty of dancing.

P.P.P.S. Chesley is a border collie mix? I love border collies—they're so smart and beautiful. I've always wanted a dog. Maybe one day…

November 10
Dear Talia—
What is this "the one" nonsense you women are always yammering about? Either you love the guy, or you don't.
Love,
Tony
P.S. Thanks for the Indian snack mix. The steam finally stopped coming out of my ears and my eyebrows are beginning to grow back. Cool! Chesley and I really enjoyed the Skittles.

Oh, and if you want a dog, get a dog! What're you waiting for?

December 2
Dear Tony—
Your ignorance appalls me! I will, however, try to put the concept into teeny-tiny words that even an ignoramus like you can understand. THE ONE is the person who provides the sunshine in your life. They bring it with them when they come, and take it with them when they leave. Duh.

That's what my friends tell me, anyway. I'm not sure I believe in the whole concept. I blame this skepticism on my father, who walked out on the family when I was about ten and my sister, Gloria, was twelve. Aren't you glad you asked?

Love,

Talia

P.S. Here is your Christmas care package, which contains six varieties of hot sauce, including the scary green ones, several hot snacks guaranteed to make your eyeballs shoot out of their sockets, and a small painting of mine called *Sol Splendor.* See the orangey bright swirls and swoops? That's the sun. This will, hopefully, let you know if you've met THE ONE. Or at least brighten a tiny corner of your wall.

P.P.S. They do provide you with a nice Christmas dinner, don't they?

Christmas Day

Dear Tony—

Sorry to overwhelm you with letters, but I am thinking about you and the other soldiers so far away from home right now. Usually I like to pretend that you're in Europe on an extended vacation, but sometimes, like today, the truth breaks through. And I worry. Since I prefer to live a laughing and carefree existence, the worrying gets to me.

Are you safe? Is your bed comfortable? Do you even have a bed, or do you sleep on some sort of horrible cot torture device? And what about your Christmas dinner? Was it any good? Was there sweet potato casserole with marshmallows?

Here is how I do my Christmas Day Extravaganza, because my motto is this: Go big, or go home—

Cinnamon candles;

Al Green's CD playing in an endless loop;

Fresh pine tree, wreaths and garland;

Gingerbread houses to decorate;

Roaring fire;

Brined turkey (I'm a fabulous cook!) with cranberry dressing;

Sweet potato casserole topped with nicely toasted marshmallows;

All (and I do mean all) the trimmings;

Pumpkin pie;

Pecan pie;

Hot chocolate with (you guessed it!) tiny marshmallows and crème de menthe; and

A viewing of *Home Alone.*

So, anyway, please let me know that you're safe and that there were some marshmallows involved in your Christmas Day experience. And I hope that next Christmas is everything you dream it will be.

Love from Talia

January 3

Dear Talia—

The painting is incredible. So was your letter. They were the best parts of my Christmas Day.

All I can say is—thank you.

Wishing you a wonderful New Year,

Tony

P.S. There was a tiny marshmallow sliver on my sweet potatoes, and the turkey was quite edible, so fear not.

P.P.S. I hope Paul appreciates how special his Christmas was.

* * *

January 17

Dear Tony—

Paul reports that his Christmas Day with his family in L.A. was lovely. I, meanwhile, had a great holiday here in NYC with my sister and friends. Paul and I are on a "break," which means that we are reevaluating our relationship and whether we want to move in together or go our separate ways. I have never been on a "break" before, so I have no idea how this will turn out.

Oh, and before I forget to mention it—don't think that I haven't noticed the way you always dodge my questions about your experience in Afghanistan. Is it that I don't have the appropriate security clearance?

I've decided to try you on something new— habanero potato chips! The store clerk had to use tongs to put them into the shopping bag, so I think they should be perfect for you!

Love,

Talia

February 10

Dear Talia—

Paul is a $%^#@ idiot. Feel free to tell him I said so. How is the break going?

I don't want to talk about the war with you. It already takes up enough of my life.

Thanks for the potato chips. They burned the fingerprints off of most of my fingers, which was way cool.

How is your work going? Do you have any fun new students? I want to hear more.

Love,

Tony

P.S. Why have you never sent me a picture?

February 25

Dear Tony—

The break is over! Paul and I are back on and looking for a two-bedroom apartment in Chelsea. Wish us luck!

I do not have any Picassos in my class this time, alas. More like several blind Jackson Pollocks. They do love to wave that paint around, but what are you going to do with five-year-olds?

Much to my surprise, I seem to be the new "it" artist right now. After I did a portrait for this one socialite/philanthropist (translation: she's richer than God), she recommended me to all her even richer friends. So now I'm overwhelmed with commissions. I've even started doing murals on the walls of some jaw-dropping apartments, which is quite the switch for me.

Basically, I have more success than I can handle at the moment, although I haven't had time to paint any of my favorite slashes and swirls in a while. Be careful what you wish for, eh?

Oh, and before I forget to mention it—I don't have any pictures to send, but I will take a couple when I get the chance.

This time: jalapeño beef jerky. Truly disgusting. Happy eating!

Gotta go. All this work is wearing me out, big-time, and I think I'm working on an infection of some sort. So I better haul my a$$ to bed....

Love,
Talia

March 25
Dear Tony—
I haven't heard back from you yet, and I'm starting to worry. I HATE worrying! And there's a lot of stuff going on around here right now, so I'd prefer to focus all my worrying energies on that.

Here are the scenarios I'm worried about with you:

1—You have thrown me aside in favor of another pen pal who sends better care packages and spicier snacks than I do;

2—The jalapeño beef jerky caused your head to explode and you are therefore unable to find a pen and write me back;

3—You are wounded.

I'm really hoping it's #1.

Even if I've somehow gotten on your nerves, please, PLEASE write back so I can find something more appropriate to worry about. And then I'll stop bugging you, okay? I'll even make it really easy for you. Just check a box:

____ Yes, I am alive
____ Other

Love,
Talia

P.S. You asked for a picture last time, and here it is: me in my studio, painting and happy.

* * *

April 10

Dear Talia—

I'm sorry for worrying you.

You are not the only one who likes to pretend the war isn't happening. There have been many nights when I lie in bed and pretend I'm just a guy with a dog and a beautiful painting of the sun to soothe away his troubles.

But the war always comes back.

Things are bad here, Talia. And getting worse daily. I look around for signs of hope, but I can't find any. Sometimes I stare at my service revolver and wonder if it wouldn't be easier to just—

Remember Chesley, our unit's bomb-sniffing K-9? She was killed when she stepped on a mine, and we all saw it happen. But I am trying to focus on this: she died on her feet, a hero, and I can only hope that when my time comes, I will do the same.

Love,

Tony

P.S. Thank you for the picture. Your smile is more beautiful than I remembered, and so are your gray eyes.

April 26

Dear Tony—

I have picked up my pen a thousand times, hoping each time that something profoundly comforting would flow from my heart and brain and onto the paper. So far, it hasn't. All I know is this: Chesley is in a better place, and now when she runs across a field, it's only a field. Not a death trap.

As for you—don't you ever let me hear you talk that way again! EVER! You are not going to die in Afghanistan. I don't care how bad things look sometimes and, trust me, I know a little about *bad.* Dying in the war is not your destiny. I can feel it.

Did I mention that I like quotes? I can whip out a quote for every occasion. So here is a Lord Byron quote to get you through the dark hours between now and when you can come home for good:

"'Tis very certain the desire of life prolongs it."

Your job, Tony, is to stay safe and desire life. Always.

Promise me?

Love,

Talia

May 17

Dear Talia—

War can't be wished away. Death can't be ignored. He stalks me everywhere I go, and is waiting around every corner for me. I'm in his shadow, and I can't get out. I escaped him today, yeah, but what about tomorrow? Is this meal my last one? This sunset? This letter? How many more of anything do I have coming to me?

This is no time for me to take anything for granted.

It's not that I regret being a soldier. Don't think

that. I'm proud of my service. I'd do it again in a heartbeat. It's just that lately I feel like I have more to lose than I've ever had before, and it has everything to do with you.

So I have a quote for you, from poet William Ross Wallace:

"Every man dies—not every man really lives."

If I could die soon—and who are we kidding; I probably WILL die soon—I don't want it to be before I really live and tell you some things you should know. With apologies to Paul, because I'm not normally a guy who tries to take something that belongs to someone else.

But, Talia—

Talia.

I think about you.

I carry you with me. Your smile is in my heart. Your name is in my head. Your face is in my dreams. It doesn't matter that we've only met face-to-face one time, or that I was engaged to someone else. I'm overflowing with you. Only you.

There. I said it. I don't expect you to say or do anything back. I just had to say it. I couldn't breathe without saying it.

Yours,

Tony

May 30

Dear Tony—

Remember this: when Death comes after you, you look him in the face and say, "Not today."

And you repeat that EVERY SINGLE DAY until you're back here, where you belong.

As for the rest of it—you have to stop, Tony. You're breaking my heart.

Talia

June 12
Sweet Talia,

I can't stop. You've gotten inside my heart. I can't get you out.

Yours,
Tony

July 11
Dear Talia—

The silence is killing me. I'm sorry. I'll never mention my feelings again. I swear. But please write to me. Something. Anything.

Tony

Tony hurried into the APO, his key at the ready in his shaky hand, and pulled up short when he saw someone—McClain, wasn't it?—already there. The kid was getting his mail out of his slot and seemed to be taking his sweet time about it. Tony hovered, growing more agitated by the second, as the kid pulled out several envelopes and rifled through them, looking for one in particular, which turned out to be a bubblegum-pink number.

Classy.

The envelope also seemed to have been drenched in several gallons of vanilla perfume, a fact that was not lost on McClain. In raptures of delight, he gave a little whoop, pressed the envelope to his nose, slammed his box shut and wheeled around with a shit-eating grin on his face.

That was when he saw Tony.

His smile withered a little. "Sorry, Captain."

Tony, who understood how important letters could be and how they held the entire universe in their folded pages, was in a mood to be sympathetic. He smiled. "Don't worry about it."

McClain hurried off, his treasures pressed to his chest, and Tony worked on getting his key into his mail slot, an effort that took three tries. He finally got the little metal door open and felt a wild swoop of relief as he peered inside and saw...

There it was!

He snatched out the single white envelope and flipped it over to work on the flap, desperate to know if Talia had forgiven him and—

Jesus.

No.

It wasn't from Talia. It was his last letter to her. And written across the envelope, in red pen in Talia's hand-writing, were the four most terrible words he could imagine reading.

Refused. Return to Sender.

A lead weight settled in his gut, so sickening and dizzying that he had to slump against the wall of mail slots to avoid dropping to the floor in an undignified heap.

That was it, then.

He'd never hear from Talia again. She had her gut feelings, but he also had his.

And right now, his gut was telling him that his

number was up. The mission tomorrow, a joint patrol with his brother's unit, was going to be his last.

There was no way he was going to make it back alive.

Chapter 1

Present day

Knowing it was a nightmare didn't make it any less terrifying.

It always started out so sweet—so achingly, indescribably sweet—and that was part of the problem. In the dream, he wasn't yet a skinny former POW struggling with PTSD and God knew what other mental deficiencies. He was still a soldier.

"You want me, don't you?" she murmured.

It was Talia. It was always Talia.

She was right there, right within the reach of his searching arms, but her face was shadowed and obscured by those flowing black curls, and, try though he did, he could only catch a flash of her laughing gray eyes. His eyes strained into the gloom, trying to see. If he could only see her, just one freaking time, he'd be the happiest man to ever put his pants on one leg at a time.

But she slipped away and the darkness edged closer.

Only her sounds guided him. The clink of her silver bracelets. The laugh, which was throaty and knowing. The seductive purr of her voice in his ear.

"You want me, don't you, Tony?"

The frustration churned inside him. He lunged for her and missed, stumbling blindly now and turning in a clumsy circle, only to realize that her low voice was coming from somewhere else—some direction he could never quite pinpoint. A place he could never reach.

"Tony? Tell me."

"I want you. You know I need you. Where are you?"

"Here."

She made it sound so easy, but it wasn't easy at all. Because he could see suddenly, and the seeing turned his bones to melting chips of ice. There she was. Far away from him, in the middle of a road in Kandahar, where it was rocky and dusty and the passing convoy of Humvees and the swooping copters overhead didn't know how precious she was.

Then the shit storm started.

Rockets and IEDs exploded, showering the whole world with shrapnel and clumps of earth so hard they could be used to cut diamonds. Men yelled and then, inevitably, screamed. The line of vehicles splintered into those trying to speed up and escape, those swerving and crashing into others, and those disintegrating into nothing between this blink and the next.

In the middle of the chaos, too far away for Tony to reach, stood Talia. He sprinted and jumped, weaving through the destruction and ignoring men who needed his help because only she mattered.

"Talia," he roared. "Talia."

She reached out her arms to him. "Here."

"Taliaaaa—"

"Come on, man," said a male voice. "Wake up."

"Taliaaaa!"

No one would stop him from getting to her. He flailed and kicked, connecting with a nose and what might have been a jaw. There was a loud yelp, and then concrete restraints locked down around him, and they had no give at all.

Not that he was giving up. He would never give up.

"No," he shouted. "Talia. Talia—"

"Tony," said that wry male voice, "I swear to God, man, if you broke my nose, I'm going to knock your teeth out. I don't care if you are dreaming."

Tony jerked awake, and it was over.

The restraints eased, allowing him to breathe again, and he opened his eyes with no real need to see anything, because the scene never changed.

It was dark, probably because it was a quarter past dead of night. He lay on his back, nested in the crawl space he made for himself every night, between the back of his bedroom sofa and the wall. The blankets were tangled and he was sweaty. He never bothered with a pillow because half the time he woke up face-down, and he hadn't made it through the war only to come home and suffocate himself like a dumbass.

And speaking of dumbasses...

His fraternal twin, Sandro, sat in his usual spot, on the floor with his back against the wall at the head of Tony's sofa, his legs bent and his feet bare. He glared, using the bottom of his white T-shirt to swipe at the blood dripping from his nostrils.

Shit.

With a harsh sigh, Tony heaved himself up into a kneeling position and started in with the apologies, which never seemed to end these days.

"Listen, man—"

Sandro waved a hand. "Forget it. I'm just glad you haven't sliced my head off."

That reminded him. Tony jerked around, rifling under the blankets for—

"Looking for this?" Sandro raised a sheathed boot knife, whose three-and-a-half-inch steel blade went a long way toward getting rid of Tony's demons in the night.

"Yeah." Tony held his hand out. "I'll take it."

Sandro shook his head and slipped it behind his back and into the elastic waistband of his plaid pajama bottoms. "Yeah…no. You won't."

Tony, who was still breathing deep to get his racing pulse under control, frowned and opened his mouth.

Whereupon Sandro emitted a low growl. "Say something," he warned.

Tony, knowing Sandro was right and that they were, after all, on the same team, shut his mouth. There were other people rattling around in the huge house—namely Sandro's teenage son, Nikolas; and Skylar, Tony's former fiancée, now Sandro's fiancée—and neither Tony nor Sandro wanted anyone to get hurt during one of Tony's frequent nocturnal meltdowns.

Things were complicated in the Davies household in the Hamptons.

Still, backing down rankled Tony, especially when

forced upon him by his marginally younger brother. "Put that thing somewhere safe," Tony told him. "I'm going to want it back."

"Don't worry." Sandro leaned his head against the wall, scrubbed a hand over his face and closed his bleary eyes. "You'll get it back the second some insurgents show up stateside and come knocking on our door."

"Funny," Tony snapped.

Sandro dropped his hand and turned to look at him with pitying eyes. "You can't go on like this, man. This is the third time this week."

Since this was likely to lead into yet another discussion about the progress—or lack thereof—Tony was making with his shrink and weekly support group of local vets who were as screwed up as he was, he decided to head the topic off at the pass.

"I know," he said. "I'm going into the city tomorrow."

Sandro's interest sharpened, probably because he was a nosy SOB and Tony had made the mistake of telling him a little about his ill-fated correspondence with Talia.

"To find her?"

Tony nodded with grim satisfaction. "Yeah."

"About damn time," Sandro muttered.

Tony couldn't argue with that.

Now that he'd made the decision that had been festering in the back of his thoughts for days now, he felt relieved to have a plan. Which was not, by the way, the same as being unafraid. Talia's rejection by return-to-sender mail all those months ago had hurt. Bad. Now here he was, heading off into the unknown and giving her another chance to hurt him.

Brilliant.

Still, he needed to see her. And, one way or the other, he needed to know if she'd ever felt anything for him. If there was any possibility of—

Nah. He wouldn't let himself go there. Not yet.

But still…it was about damn time.

"I'll be gone a couple days. I'll stay at the penthouse. And I'll check in with Marcus and Cooper." Their cousins ran the auction house full-time. "I've had enough downtime already. It's time for me to get to work. Resume my rightful place with Davies & Sons."

Sandro raised a brow. "Marcus and Cooper will love that."

Tony managed a tired but amused snort. "Screw them."

They sat in silence for a minute, but then Sandro snapped his fingers. "What about Arianna? She's supposed to be coming in for a visit."

"I know." As if there was any chance Tony would forget the impending visit from their younger sister and her growing family.

"She's bringing the baby and Joshua."

"I know."

"Well, you need to make sure you check in with her and make sure we all get our schedules synced," Sandro said darkly. "I'm not trying to get killed. And don't forget I'm heading down to D.C. with Nikolas and Skylar. We need to get working on the house hunting." Sandro had recently accepted a position at the Pentagon as an analyst and would be moving soon. "In fact, it might be easier if you postpone your little NYC jaunt until—"

Fueled by impatience, Tony surged to his feet and strode across the room to his closet, where he kept his duffel bag. It may have been the middle of the night, but there was no time like the present to put his plan into action, and he wasn't in the mood for chitchat.

"No," he said. "I'm not trying to work around anyone's schedule. This is too important. I'm finished waiting. It's past time for me to see Talia."

By about ten-thirty that morning, after riding the train into Penn Station and the subway down to the Village (he hated taxis, limos, driving in the city and traffic delays, not necessarily in that order), Tony found himself in front of the converted warehouse where Talia rented studio space.

He loitered outside the heavy metal security door, some of his excitement tampered by stark terror. Having spent a lot of time in fear while he was in Afghanistan, he recognized it when he saw it, and this was it. His pulse raced; his hands trembled; beneath his armpits he felt the slow trickle of clammy sweat.

Hell, he could almost laugh about it. Maybe the war hadn't caused his raging PTSD after all. Maybe its source was the loss of the woman he'd never even had.

But not like it mattered why he was batshit crazy.

Whatever. He might be crazy, but he wasn't a coward, and this was the moment of truth when he could prove it. So he raised his finger and pressed the buzzer, giving it a nice long ring.

No answer, but the place was a cavern and it probably took a good two minutes for someone to walk down the hall and reach the door.

He waited, turning to face the street's bustle, with its usual assortment of hurrying New Yorkers talking on their cell phones, disposable coffee cups snuggled close to their chests.

Overhead, the sky was a chilly slate-gray that belonged in November rather than May, but he didn't feel the cold. He was way too hopped-up on adrenaline to be affected by anything as insignificant as the weather, and his jacket was—

Without warning, the door swung open. Tony found himself confronted by a woman about his age—mid-thirties—with a flat-lined mouth and lowered brows that told him he'd already pissed her off and anything further he did—like, say, speaking—would only worsen the situation. Brown-skinned with sleek black hair and sharp brown eyes that surely missed nothing, she would have been pretty but for the overdose of bad attitude and harsh black-on-black clothes.

"Can I help you?" she demanded.

"I, ah," he began, hoping she didn't decide to haul off and hit him, "I'd like to see Talia Adams."

The woman was not impressed. "Do you have an appointment?"

"No."

"And you are…?"

"Tony Davies."

"What's the nature of your business?"

He was starting to get annoyed. He knew of several high-security government buildings that were easier to access than this place.

"I'm a friend. Is she here?"

Miss Personality narrowed her eyes. "Don't take that tone with me. I'll ask if she'll see you."

"Thanks ever so much."

Another glare, and then she pivoted and headed off down the hall, leaving him to lunge for the heavy door and squeak inside before it could swing shut in his face.

Not the auspicious beginning he'd hoped for, clearly, but Talia was here, in the same building, and that was all that mattered. He hurried after the black-clad woman and followed her up a flight of stairs, dodging a well-dressed couple who were directing a man with a boxy marble sculpture on a dolly, and a gaggle of elementary school kids being herded by their frazzled-looking teacher. They passed the doors—some open and some closed—of other studios, and then they were outside the final door on the left.

The door.

Talia Adams said the sign. *Painter.*

The woman strode inside the studio with no understanding of how important this moment was to Tony, or how he'd lived for it, calling as she went, "Tally? Where you at, girl? Tally? Talia!"

Tony waited on the threshold, incapable of breathing.

Nothing happened.

The woman turned back and shrugged, ignorant of his turmoil, which was a very good thing. "Guess she went to the bathroom. You can wait if you want."

"Great."

"Great." The woman reached for a cardboard box and shot him a last warning frown. "Don't get in the way."

"Wouldn't dream of it."

He looked around, reveling in Talia's presence and getting his bearings, but things didn't feel quite right. There was one jarring difference between the studio of his memory and this one: the open cardboard boxes everywhere announced that Talia was in the middle of a move.

This possibility, he discovered, didn't sit well with him. What if she was headed to Paris for a year of study or something similar?

On the other hand, what if she was now married to Paul?

That possibility damn near gave him chills, so he decided to pretend that Paul had never existed, at least until he was presented with undeniable evidence to the contrary.

' The studio was still stark and bright, though, with high ceilings, exposed pipes and beams, and a wall of paneled windows that looked out on the street below and let in every available glimmer of sunlight. There were drop cloths and drafting tables, the sharp smell of turpentine, and canvases of various sizes and shapes leaning against the walls.

The work was as brilliant as he remembered; he'd spent enough time studying art history in school and paintings at the auction house over the years to recognize a talented artist when he encountered one, and Talia was the real deal.

She had two portraits on easels. Were these her most recent works, then? The first was of a smiling woman with brown-and-white spaniels sitting on her lap. The colors were sharp and vibrant, and Talia had captured the woman's personality in the amused quirk of her mouth. The dogs, meanwhile, had their ears cocked and looked restless, as though they'd been promised a chicken treat if they only sat still long enough to be captured on canvas.

The other portrait was of a mother and her toddler son, their heads bent low over a collection of wooden alphabet blocks as they built a tower.

He stopped and stared, awed and lost in the details of the nursery, the strands of gold in the woman's tumbling red hair, her freckles and the rosy glow of the toddler's fat cheeks.

"She's good, isn't she?" Miss Personality, who was now standing at a workstation on the other side of the studio, putting items into one of the cardboard boxes, favored him with the beginnings of a smile.

"She's amazing."

He meandered, studying another collection of paintings, some leaning and some hanging on the walls. These were explosions of glowing color representing all kinds of things, as though Talia had painted an item, deconstructed it and put it back together using shapes, slashes and swirls that were infinitely more interesting than the original.

A field of flowers. A forest. A barn. Seashells.

And then, on another wall, a different collection that was as dark and forbidding as the others were warm and vivid. These paintings didn't seem to represent anything other than all the ways that colors could come together and form…night. Despair. The complete absence of light.

He stared while dread crawled up his spine with prickly feet.

The change was extraordinary, as though he'd been inside a rainbow, blinked and discovered that he'd been sucked into the malevolent heart of a black hole. It seemed impossible that the same person could have produced all these different moods. Why would she paint such heartbreak? What had happened to her? He hated the idea of Talia occupying such a dismal place, even temporarily, and even if only in her imagination.

"What happened here?" he asked the woman, pointing to a dark painting that probably had a title like Tornado in Hell or Hope Screams Bloody Murder. "I don't get why these are so different—"

Without warning, the door banged open again and a woman swept into the room, bringing the energy of ten people with her.

Tony froze.

His heart also clanged to a stop.

"I think we should work on the acrylics next, Glo," the woman announced in the whiskey-smooth voice that'd been haunting his thoughts for as long as he could remember. "I won't be needing them for a while— Oh, who's this?"

Jesus. His brain emptied out, leaving him paralyzed and dumb.

Talia—there she finally was.

She went utterly still, as undone by the moment as he was.

Their gazes locked and held, and her gray eyes slowly went wide with astonishment. A flush crept over her light brown cheeks, making her look feverish, and her lush berry mouth dropped open in a gape.

Moving like a sleepwalker, she edged closer to study him better, and her fragrance teased his nose. She wore a feminine cocktail of something fruity, and he was surprised to find that forgotten detail about her now so electrifying.

And her bracelets…

Those silver bangles he'd teased her about, a thousand or so of them on her left arm, clinked gently as she walked. He felt such a rush of swelling joy it was as though his entire life had been nothing more than a prelude to this moment.

He stared, gathering up all of her quirks and features so he'd never forget anything about her ever again.

She was shorter and thinner than he'd remembered, her cheeks sharper, and she had that same collection of silver earrings marching up her lobes. Her long, summery dress was flowered and left her toned arms bare, and a quick downward glance revealed flat sandals, toe rings and white nail polish at the tips of her pretty feet.

Her hair, which had been black with springy haywire curls, was straight and pixie-short now, and—holy shit—blue. Not blue-black, either, but the electric-blue of a stove's gas flame. He wasn't a fan of rainbow colors when it came to hair, but the effect on her was oddly appropriate.

Bottom line?

She was more beautiful than the images he'd hoarded in his memory bank.

"Tony?" she breathed.

"Yeah," he said gruffly, reaching for her.

"Oh, my God."

They came together hard and fast, and then, for the first time ever, she was in his arms, and he couldn't hold her tight enough.

Chapter 2

Tony lifted her until only her toes grazed the floor, marveling at the perfect fit, the warmth and solidity of her, and the silky slide of the dress over her supple body. Her skin was a delicious combination of satin and velvet, and he buried his face in the sweet hollow between her neck and shoulder and inhaled, desperate to experience her with all of his senses.

"Tony." Her voice cracked and overflowed with emotion. *"Tony."*

"Wow." Miss Personality's dry voice intruded. "I'm guessing you two really do know each other."

Way to break the spell, he thought.

Self-conscious and awkward now, Tony lowered Talia to her feet but kept an arm on her back because he needed the contact. Apparently, she didn't. Stepping out of his grasp, she smoothed her hair and made a real project of avoiding his gaze.

"So," he said.

"So," Talia echoed. "You've met my sister, right?"

Sister? "Not exactly."

Talia flashed a dimple, but her smile never quite took hold. "Gloria Adams, this is Captain Antonios Davies."

"Tony," he said quickly, extending his hand.

Gloria's appraising gaze, which was considerably more interested in him than it had been a minute ago, swept over him as they shook hands.

"Captain? Are you a marine, or—"

He shuddered. "God forbid. I'm army. Well, was. I've been discharged."

The interrogation continued. "Honorable, or—"

"Gloria," Talia snapped.

"It's okay," he told her. "Honorable. Would you like to see my discharge papers?"

"Do you have them?" Gloria asked sweetly.

"Yeah, okay." Talia hooked her elbow onto Gloria's, marched her to the door and shoved her into the hall. "It's time for you to go do that thing you needed to do."

Gloria pulled a bewildered expression, but the amused glimmer in her eye didn't fool anyone. "What thing?"

"That. Thing."

Tony caught a glimpse of Gloria opening her mouth to argue, but then Talia closed the door in her sister's face with a decisive snap.

Thank God, he thought, his pulse kicking into overdrive.

Alone at last.

"Sorry about that." Talia took her time coming back,

and he had the feeling she was stalling. She had her fingers laced together in a white-knuckled grip that betrayed her nerves, and this, strangely, made him feel better, as he also felt as though he was drowning in awkwardness. "Nosy big sister and all."

"It's okay."

They stared at each other, their breathing still uneven. Her face remained flushed, and his felt so hot he could fry bacon on his forehead.

Words overflowed from his heart, but he couldn't get any of them to his mouth. He'd thought that after all this time of wanting *this*—to be in the same room with her again—he'd have prepared a sentence or two, but nothing seemed to fit this moment.

"It's great to see you," he finally said.

"You, too."

More staring ensued.

She had a perfect round mole at the corner of her mouth, and her eyes tipped up at the corners. The dimple in her left cheek was more pronounced than the one in her right. Her eyes were more silvery than gray; why hadn't he remembered that?

This cataloguing of her features showed signs of outlasting the Ice Age, but then she finally blinked and remembered her duties as a hostess.

"We should sit."

"Yeah," he agreed, trying to get his head in the game. "Sit. Good idea."

He followed her to a sofa in front of one of the windows, where she perched on the edge. Since he wanted to face her, he sat on the trunk that apparently doubled as a coffee table, rested his elbows on his knees and took a deep breath.

"I should have called first," he told her.

"It's okay."

"I didn't mean to surprise you."

Her eyes crinkled at the corners, further scrambling his thoughts. "Wonderful surprises are okay."

"I'm, ah…I'm not dead."

"That explains the whole walking and talking thing."

He grinned, wondering when he'd last been this ridiculously inarticulate in a female's presence. Sixth grade? "What I mean is—"

"I read about your 'death' in the paper. And then a few weeks ago I read in the paper about your being a POW. It's a miracle that you escaped and made it back safely."

"Oh," he said, faltering.

Nothing chopped a man's ego down to size quicker than knowing that the woman he wanted was so disinterested in the news of his resurrection that she hadn't bothered to call or write. But of course she'd already made her position clear with that return-to-sender letter, hadn't she?

Still, it hurt. Like a spiked wrecking ball to his gut.

He was a big boy, though, and he'd get over it. He hadn't come all this way, physically and emotionally, to just go away quietly and give up on the idea of exploring a romantic relationship with her.

"So, yeah, I've been home for about a month."

"Your brother and sister must be so thrilled."

Did that mean that *she* wasn't thrilled? "They are."

A shadow crossed her face, telling him what was coming next. "Are you okay? I mean—physically?"

"Yes."

"I'm glad."

"Are you?" he asked.

He wasn't normally the needy type, but then he wasn't normally interested in a woman who knew if he was dead or alive only by reading the papers. Despite all his stern internal lectures about not getting his hopes up, he'd done exactly that, nursing all kinds of glorious reunion scenarios that ended with them tumbling into the nearest bed for a long and urgent interlude of getting-to-know-you.

That probably wasn't going to happen.

Big surprise, right?

Worse, her growing polite coolness and his old familiar feeling of dread—he was always dreading something—had him in a stranglehold.

"Are you glad, I mean?" he continued.

"Yes."

Her unabashed vehemence made him lose his head a little, and he reached for her. "Talia."

He heard the husky vulnerability in his voice, but nothing mattered except the feel of her beautiful face between his palms—Christ, her skin was soft—and the need to feel her mouth moving against his. Her melting little sigh made his heart ache. He ducked his head, drowning in lust and need, and tipped her chin up to—

"I can't." At the very last second, she stiffened and turned away.

He was beyond hearing, so he didn't let her go.

Talia...Talia...Talia...

Grabbing his wrists, she pulled free of his hands. *"I can't."*

Tony reined himself in, hard, even though he'd waited so long and moved heaven and earth to arrive at this moment, and even though the flashing turbulence in her eyes didn't match her sharp tone.

It took him a good long time to wrestle his frustration into submission, and longer to get past the delicious sensation of touching her skin.

"You can't?" he echoed dully.

"No."

"Because of Paul?"

Her brows contracted with bewilderment. "Paul?"

He reached for her left hand and pulled it out where he could examine it. She wore a silver butterfly ring, but no wedding band, so that was good. Great, actually.

Still, the idea of having lost her forever while the Taliban had kept him hostage and helpless turned his heart to stone.

"Did you marry him?" he demanded.

"What? No."

That was a small step in the right direction. "But you're still together?"

"No."

"There's someone else?"

"No, Tony—"

He stared at her; she kept her head bowed.

Deep inside, he felt that snake's nest of dread twist and writhe.

"Help me out, then. I don't understand."

"There's nothing to understand." She hesitated, shrugging. "You're making assumptions. That's the problem."

Assumptions?

He supposed he was. Hell. Wasn't this whole trip down to the Village to see her all about one giant assumption?

And yet…

She was into him, too. He knew it. He could feel it.

Straining his brain, he tried to think of the letter—the exact paragraph, sentence and words—where she'd admitted she had feelings for him. She had said it, hadn't she? Why couldn't he remember? Why had he taken her precious letters with him that last day, tucked inside his vest pocket for luck? Luck. Yeah. Funny. Luck hadn't saved him from being captured, and it hadn't saved his letters, which had probably been kindling for some insurgent's fire.

Now he couldn't reread them and find the proof he needed.

Oh, but it got worse.

In this cold light of a May day, months later, he had to admit that it was possible he'd imagined something between the lines of her letters—something that had never been there.

Had he imagined her tenderness?

Was he that deluded, on top of the PTSD?

No, something shouted inside him.

Where did the absolute certainty come from? Maybe it was that crawling gut instinct that had repeatedly kept him alive during the war, or maybe he was just insane, pure and simple.

"Talia." He chose his words carefully, afraid of getting everything wrong and driving her away by sounding like an arrogant jackass. "I thought we were developing something."

She nodded, her gaze now fixed on some immovable point to the right of his eyes. "We were. Friendship. That's all. I don't have romantic feelings for you."

Bullshit, screamed his gut instinct. Inside him, the frustration rose.

"That's all?"

"Yes."

"If it's that cut-and-dried, why aren't you looking at me?"

That got her. Her gaze flickered to her fingers, which were twined and buried in her lap, then to his collar. She opened and closed her mouth. Opened it again. Finally looked into his eyes.

The utter darkness he saw there made him flinch. It was like staring into one of her black hole paintings. It leached the soul out of his body and left nothing but emptiness.

"I don't want a relationship right now, Tony. I'm not sure I'll ever want one. I don't have room in my life—"

"Why not?"

Her mouth worked and worked, but no words came out.

"Why not?"

"I'm taking time off from work. I want to travel. I've hardly been anywhere in my life—"

"Travel, then. I'd never try to stop you from doing what you want to do, Talia—"

"—and I just… I can't handle any complications right now."

"Wow. That's pretty much everything and the kitchen sink. Anything else?"

Her brows contracted into an indignant line. "Is this a cross-examination? Am I on trial? Is that what's going on?"

"You're not on trial. But I don't believe anything you

just said. Especially the part about not having feelings for me."

She nailed him with a glare that nearly made his face bleed. "Nice. Arrogant, much?"

Brilliant, Davies.

He ran a hand over his nape, trying hard to arrange his features into an expression that felt less intense. "I'm sorry. It's just that…" He fumbled, struggling for words that kept skittering just out of reach. If he'd cut out his tongue with his boot knife, the conversation still would have been easier than this. "I can't stop thinking about you. Your letters meant so much to me. And then when you refused the last one—"

"I didn't think it was fair for me to give you mixed messages. That's why I sent it back. You were reading too much into it."

Funny she should mention mixed messages.

He stared into her face, seeing her turbulence, and he felt the ghostly imprint of her body fitted perfectly against his. He heard the echoes of her joyful cry when she had first seen him just now, and of her needy sigh when he'd almost kissed her.

Most of all, he remembered the unspoken subtext of longing in her letters.

Weighing all of that against her unimpressive denials, he decided that, while he might well be crazy, it was more likely that she was a liar.

Since he couldn't figure out why she would lie if she wasn't involved with someone else, he felt the first twinges of anger.

"You're pretty good at giving mixed messages, Talia."

Something flashed in her eyes, and he couldn't tell

if it was anger, fear or garden variety turmoil. He was still struggling to make sense of this giant and incomprehensible puzzle when she speared him right through the heart with the worst possible weapon against him.

"They were only letters, Tony," she said coolly. "I'd've done the same for any soldier."

Drenched in sweat and arms pumping, Tony sprinted around the Reservoir in Central Park for the third time, which meant he was flirting with three miles so far. He'd need at least three more before he had any hope of quieting the relentless chatter in his head, so he kept going, working harder and crashing through all the limits of his endurance. His lungs burned; his thighs screamed; his heart was a frantic beat or two away from exploding out of his chest.

On the one hand, the workout was an excruciating punishment, bordering on torture. On the other hand, this was the perfect exercise to keep the rising frustration at bay.

It was either run or throw back his head and roar until his head cleared.

Since he didn't fancy an involuntary trip to Bellevue for overnight evaluation, he ran.

They were only letters, Tony. I'd've done the same for any soldier.

That's what Talia had told him. Translation? He wasn't special, and the shared connection forged through those letters had been a beautiful mirage carved out of his overactive imagination, nothing more.

So that was it, then.

That was the end of his crazy fantasies about Talia falling into his arms and then…

What, Tony? asked a mocking little voice inside his head.

What, exactly, did you see happening then?

He squinted and strained, trying to get his mind's eye to focus a little, maybe tell him what it'd had in mind for him and Talia, but he couldn't see it, and it didn't matter anyway. Whatever it was, it wouldn't happen. Ever.

His feet pounding, he dodged and wove, avoiding strollers, walkers and other joggers, all of whom were moving too slow and needed to get the hell out of his way.

He'd wanted to know whether he and Talia had a chance. Now he knew, and, though the knowledge was painful, it was better than not knowing.

Well, no. He'd already known, hadn't he? *What else could that refused letter have meant, dumbshit? I'm waiting for you with open arms?* Yeah, right. He should've saved himself the train fare for the humiliating trip into the city, but, oh well. Lesson learned, and better late than never. The end.

That's what he told himself, anyway.

Deep inside, though, he couldn't force himself to accept it.

Which was why he kept running.

He was rounding the curve nearest the Metropolitan Museum of Art when his cell phone vibrated inside his shorts pocket. Thinking—desperately hoping—it might be Talia, he snatched it, punched the button and had it up to his ear before he remembered: *she doesn't have your cell number.*

Dumbshit.

"Yeah," he snarled, still running.

"This is your sister," answered Arianna's dry voice.

While this was better than a call from, say, the IRS with concerns about his most recent tax return, he still wasn't in a mood for talking. "Hey."

"Have I offended you somehow?"

Right now, the whole stinking world offended him.

"Nope," he said, swerving around a dog that was sniffing at his legs, wanting to say hi as he passed.

"Because you don't sound too happy to hear my lovely voice."

"Sorry," he puffed. "Bad morning."

"What're you doing? Hauling logs?"

"Jogging. In Central Park."

"Um…okay. I feel like I should hang up and get 9-1-1 on the line…"

"I'll be okay. What's up?"

There was a long pause. "I was just checking in. I don't want to take the baby on any airplanes just yet with all those rampant germs, so I think it'll be another week or so before we're ready to come visit, sunshine. At which point I hope you have a better attitude than the one you have now."

That did it. Few things had ever brought him to heel like a guilt trip from Arianna, with whom he'd always been close. They'd had a joyous reunion a few weeks ago, right after his return from overseas, when he'd flown to Columbus to see her after the birth of her first child, a daughter. Arianna didn't deserve his gruffness. God knew she wasn't the one who'd smashed his hopes to bits.

"Sorry." He slowed down and dropped onto the nearest empty bench, where he doubled up and tried to get his breath. "It's not your fault I'm being a, ah—"

"Grouchy SOB?" she supplied helpfully. "What's got you all bent out of shape?"

He opened his mouth and out popped the automatic denial. "It's nothing."

"Hmm." Arianna, as usual, read between the lines and came up with the right answer. If he believed in reincarnation, he'd put his money on her having been a bloodhound in a past life. "Or should I say, who's got you all bent out of shape?"

He sat back, hung his arm across the back of the bench and drummed his fingers, thinking about this for a minute. He wasn't in the habit of discussing his personal life with his sister, but his personal life had previously consisted of brief sexual relationships with women who didn't expect anything from him other than a nice dinner and a few orgasms.

In short, he'd never had an issue like Talia before.

But he had to face it—Arianna was a smart woman who had the additional qualification of being happily married. Tony still had a reservation or two about the neck-tattoo-sporting dude she'd chosen (Tony had a couple tats himself, but, come on, on the *neck?*), but that was an issue for another day.

For now, maybe she could help his ass out.

"So there's this, ah, woman."

"Yay!" Hearing the distinct sound of hand clapping, Tony rolled his eyes and waited for her to get a grip. "Where do you know her from?"

"We met before my last tour, and we exchanged a few letters."

"And...?"

"And I thought we were, ah, making a connection or

something, but when I, ah, made a, ah... When I mentioned my feelings, she, ah—"

"Wow. And here I thought English was your first language. So she's not that into you, right?"

Tony swiped his dripping face with the bottom of his T-shirt and struggled to put his thoughts into words. "That's just it. I thought she was into me."

"What made you think that?"

"I don't have objective proof. That's the problem. I just have my gut feelings, which don't count for anything. But this morning, when I went to see her, there was a second when I thought—"

"How did she look when she saw you? Don't think about it—just blurt it out."

"Overjoyed," he said. "She looked as thrilled as I was."

"Hmm." Arianna lapsed into a thoughtful silence that made his nerves stretch with impatience. "Is she involved with someone else?"

"She says she's not. She claims she's too busy with her career and stuff. She's an artist."

"Hmm." More silence. "Is she a lesbian?"

"No." He dismissed this possibility out of hand. He could compete with another man if he had to, but if what Talia really needed from a romantic partner was a vagina, then he was out of luck. "She's not gay."

"You sure?"

"Positive," he lied.

"Okay, well, then the answer's simple. She's scared."

"*Scared?* Of what?"

"You. The way you make her feel. The way she feels about you."

"Bullshit," he said, but already the wheels were turning in his mind, and he couldn't help but wonder if there was something to it. "Why would she be scared of me?"

Arianna heaved a long and exasperated sigh. "Oh, come on. Who wouldn't want a hot guy like you showing up on their doorstep? You're incredibly sexy—"

Astonished to hear his sister talking like this, Tony jerked the phone away from his ear and stared at it.

"—and she probably figures you can have any woman you want. I'm betting she's afraid of getting hurt. Plus, maybe she's already been hurt by someone—"

His mind darted to the faceless Paul, whom he'd never liked.

"—and she doesn't want to go down that road again. It's your job to figure out what's scaring her. If you care enough, that is."

Oh, he cared.

He struggled with this hypothesis. He couldn't rule out the possibility that she was secretly wild about him.

"Well, that's a brilliant theory, Sherlock," he said, "but maybe you had it right the first time. Maybe she's just not that into me."

"I see. So during your time in Afghanistan, you lost all your abilities to read a woman's signals. Is that it?"

"I'm just saying that it's possible that—"

"Oh, please."

"I'm not a stalker, Ari. She's said no, and I—"

"You give up? Really? Starting when?"

That hit a nerve, especially after his experiences as a POW.

Something inside him hardened with determination. "I don't quit."

"Good. I'm not suggesting you drag her off against her will, by the way."

"Good to know."

"I'm just saying that for once in your life, you might have to work a little harder to get the woman you want. That's all."

"But—"

"Oh, for God's sake, Tony!" she snapped. "Does the woman want you or not? Yes or no?"

"Yes," came the honest and immediate answer. "She wants me. I can feel it."

"Then figure it out."

"Oh, figure it out. Brilliant. And how am I supposed to do that, O wise one? My suggestion box is open."

"No idea. But you'll think of something. Mama, God rest her soul, and I didn't raise you to be a fool when it comes to women."

That ringing endorsement made Tony laugh for the first time in hours.

Chapter 3

Talia was already at the studio the next morning, looking at the brochures her travel agent had given her, when Gloria arrived, half an hour early. Although she was wearing a familiar expression of grim concern, she had armed herself with coffee and for Talia, her favorite daily treat: a jumbo cappuccino with extra foam and extra cinnamon. Without a word, she handed it to Talia, who flashed her a grateful smile. These days, Talia was happy for any fortification she could get, and it didn't matter if it was emotional or caloric.

They leaned against the nearest worktable and sipped for a few minutes. Then Gloria, who'd miraculously managed to delay the questioning till this moment, launched into the inevitable interrogation.

"What gives?"

Shrugging, Talia tried to keep it light and airy, which

would have been an easier proposition if her sister hadn't known her so well. "Tony's a friend. I met him when he picked up his nephew from one of my classes. He was about to return overseas. I wrote to him."

Gloria waited for the rest, brows raised.

"He was presumed dead for a while," Talia added.

"He ain't dead."

"Nope."

More silent sipping ensued. Gloria stared at her.

"What?" Talia demanded, her nerves fraying at the edges. "That's it."

No one did skeptical like Gloria. She had a way of giving her lips a derisive twist that said it all. "That's it?" she said dubiously.

"That's. It."

"Bullshit," Gloria pronounced.

"Okay." Talia slammed her cup down, shoved away from the table and, flustered, looked around for the catalogue on African safaris. "You know what? This conversation is over. *O-V-E-R.* In other news, I'm thinking about Kenya—"

"Here's what I don't get," said Gloria, who had never yet allowed a discussion to end before she had the last word. "Why are you so upset? You've barely said two words since Tony left. If it's so cut-and-dried, and there's nothing to you seeing your pen pal—" she made quotation marks with her fingers "—again, what's the big deal?"

"There's no big deal," Talia lied.

Once again, Gloria waited.

Once again, the pressure-filled silence caused Talia to blather when she should have kept her big fat mouth shut. "Well, okay, he wants to be more than friends, but that's not a good idea. For obvious reasons."

"Right. Because he's obviously a troll."

Well, there it was. Tony's physical appearance had made an impression on Gloria.

It'd made quite the impression on Talia, too.

Tall and dark-skinned, with the clean-shaven, hard-jawed, square-shouldered look of a man's man—a military man—Tony was leaner than he'd been the only other time she'd seen him, but was still blessed with the perfect amount of toned muscle and butt power. He'd worn crisp khakis and a blinding white tunic, a summery combination that brought to mind ocean breezes, rum drinks and slow-swinging hammocks. He was vital and intense, strung tight with an energy that emanated from his brown eyes and filled the air around him.

Captain Antonios Davies was, in short, a walking, talking, breathing jolt of electricity to the female body.

That didn't mean that Talia wanted to get involved with him.

Well, she wanted to, of course, but she *wouldn't.*

"Talia." Gloria waved a hand in front of her face and clicked her fingers a couple of times. "Focus, girl. Snap out of it."

"Okay, look," Talia said, seriously annoyed now. Why did she have to explain herself to the person who should understand her reasons better than anyone else on the planet? "There's an attraction there. I admit it. But I think I have enough going on in my life without—"

Gloria gave her a wide-eyed look of incomprehension. "What's going on in your life, exactly?"

Talia lost it, which was probably the whole point.

"I've got things to accomplish! You know this! I'm taking time off to travel, and I—"

"Is this about Paul?" Gloria interrupted quietly, ignoring the tirade.

"What? No! Of course not!"

"He broke your heart."

Talia tried that on for size and decided it didn't fit. "No. I was hurt, but he didn't break my heart. Actually, he did me a favor by bailing on me before things went any further, right? So let's just call it a lesson learned."

"What was the lesson?"

Talia thought about Paul, and this, naturally, bled into thoughts of her father. He was a prominent surgeon who'd walked out on their mother for the greener pastures of his twenty-two-year-old medical transcriptionist. These experiences had led Talia to one inescapable lesson: "Men can't be counted on when the going gets tough."

"I knew it!" Gloria's eyes gleamed bright with triumph. "Don't lump all men together with Paul—"

"And Dad," Talia reminded her.

"Right, right—forget Dad. My point is that Tony seemed like a good guy. And he seemed like he was really interested in you. So give him a chance. Go out for drinks. See what happens. Have some fun. I'm telling you, I've got a good feeling about him."

Talia couldn't believe her ears. "A *good feeling?* Is this the same kind of *good feeling* that led you into your ongoing two-year affair with a married man?"

Talia regretted the words as soon as they were out of her mouth, especially as Gloria winced and turned the vivid purple of a beet. Talia tried to backtrack.

"I didn't mean—"

A ghostly smile flickered across Gloria's face. "You meant it."

Talia put a hand on Gloria's arm and gave her a sympathetic squeeze. "Look. I guess the bottom line is that we both want the best for each other. I think we'll have to agree to disagree on what *the best* is."

Gloria never went down without a fight. "Tony might be the best for you. I know Aaron is the best for me."

Oh, for God's sake. Talia smacked her own forehead in frustration, wondering why Gloria needed the same blast of brutal truth over and over again.

"If Aaron wanted the best for you, he wouldn't be smuggling you to Brooklyn hotels every time he wanted to see you, and I'm guessing he *probably* wouldn't have kept you dangling for two good childbearing years with promises to leave his wife."

This clear-eyed analysis, predictably, made Gloria furious. "He's leaving her over Memorial Day weekend," she shouted. "You know he is! Why do you keep—"

Talia held up her hands and surrendered to the queen of denial. "Fine. You win. You win! Subject dropped."

Gloria, who wasn't quite ready to forgive and forget, got up in Talia's face. "You'll be eating those words soon, and I'll be expecting an apology."

"I'll be happy to apologize," Talia reassured her. "What I can't do is stay with you and hold your hand through another night of crying over that bastard."

Wrong choice of words. Again. Gloria's eyes welled up and overflowed, and she swiped angrily at the tears. "I don't need you to—"

"Sorry. One of the other tenants let me in, so I came on up."

The male voice made them both jump, and they whirled around to discover Tony peering around the ajar door. His concerned gaze went directly to Talia and latched on, and his cheeks flushed with what looked like the kind of heightened awareness that she was feeling. If he knew Gloria was also in the room, he gave no sign of it.

"You okay?" he asked.

Flustered more by his unexpected arrival than by her argument with Gloria, Talia shrugged and tried to look okay. "Of course."

They stared at each other for a lengthy beat, during which all of Talia's nerve endings sparked to attention and her lungs emptied of air. She waited, reminding herself that this unholy reaction to Tony's presence was the number one reason why she needed to stay the hell away from him. Despite what Gloria had said, this wasn't a man with whom one had fun. This was a man a woman could fall for and love until her dying day.

"I didn't mean to interrupt." Unsmiling, he came inside the studio, bringing all of his laser-sharp intensity with him. "But I need to talk to you for a minute, Talia."

Oh, no.

"Talk?" Talia echoed stupidly.

"It's important," Tony added.

Talia stared at him, all her mental wheels spinning at top speed. Any more talking was out of the question, clearly. What good could possibly come of it? They'd talked already, and her heart was still achy from the experience. Plus, every time she saw him, it got that much harder to focus on why starting a relationship with him would inevitably lead to disaster. So the answer was clear: no more talking. Talking was bad.

She opened her mouth to tell him he needed to leave. "Talk? Sure," she said.

From the corner of her eye, she saw Gloria stifle a triumphant grin behind a tiny cough, which only added to Talia's discomfort. She so did not need comments from the peanut gallery right now. Trying to be subtle about it, Talia shot Gloria a sidelong glare. Gloria, thankfully, took the hint and bustled around with a couple of boxes, trying to look busy.

Talia noticed she kept her ear cocked, though.

Filled with grim dread and making a mental note to clean Gloria's clock at the first opportunity, Talia faced Tony again and discovered him studying the top of her head.

"What're you looking at?"

Caught, he didn't deny staring. "Your hair's, ah, purple."

His unabashed interest made Talia feel self-conscious, and that, in turn, made her defiant. Glowering, she smoothed the nape of her pageboy bob, which had flat bangs and sharp angles that framed her cheeks.

"You don't like purple?"

His mouth eased into a smile that was both crooked and appreciative, and his teasing murmur was for her alone. "I love purple, but the blue worked for me, too. I can't wait to see what you come up with next."

Yeah, okay, she thought, flushing until she felt her skin sizzle.

That was not the kind of thing she needed to hear if she wanted to keep her wits about her and her feet on the ground. That was the kind of dizzying compliment guaranteed to make her foolish heart flutter, and her willpower was at an ebb so low she couldn't do much to protect herself.

Still, she tried.

"Thanks." Squaring her shoulders, she strove for a tone that was crisp and direct. This was her territory, right? Which meant that she was in control here, even though her innards had turned to lukewarm Jell-O. "What brings you back so soon?"

He wasn't listening.

With growing dismay, she watched as he turned back to the door and waved two men into the studio from the hallway. Being in the army had given him a decisive air she couldn't hope to match, or maybe he'd been born that way. Whatever the reason, none of them seemed to have any doubt about who was in charge.

So much for her being in control of this little visit, she thought sourly.

"Talia Adams," Tony said, "I'd like you to meet my cousins, Marcus Davies and his brother, Cooper. They're my partners in the auction house."

Two of the biggest names in the New York art world? Here? In her unworthy little studio? No. Freaking. Way. This could not be happening.

Scraping her jaw up off the floor, she arranged her lips into what she hoped was a casual smile, as if this sort of thing happened to her so often it was yawn worthy.

She knew who they were, of course, although they'd never met. As a working artist, it was her business to study the local players, and she'd seen countless photos of them in local magazines over the years. They wined, dined and traded in the art world the way Martha Stewart made her way around a kitchen, and here Talia was, trying to cobble together a cupcake or two. She was up and coming, yeah, but she'd figured she had to work, at the very least, several more years before these two would know she existed.

What the heck was going on? Had Christmas come early this year?

It didn't help that they were, next to Tony, two of the hottest men she'd ever seen in person. Marcus had a deep olive complexion, short, sandy hair sun-streaked with gold, amber eyes and swooping brows. He had the kind of sexy mustache and stubble that suggested he only shaved when the mood struck, which wasn't very often. His smile was easy and he was dressed in the black-on-black outfit—dress shirt with expensive jeans—that a lot of New Yorkers favored.

Cooper, Marcus's adopted brother, on the other hand, wore frayed camouflage cargo pants, a plain white T-shirt, and had an explosion of silky blond curls ringing his head like a halo. His hard jaw and thinned lips gave him the look of a man you didn't want to piss off, and his glittering blue eyes were rock hard, as though they'd been chiseled straight from sapphires.

They looked, in short, like models escaped from the pages of *GQ* and *Soldier of Fortune* magazines, respectively.

Marcus stuck out a hand and shook Talia's in his firm grip. "Talia. I'm familiar with your work. We thought it was time to take a closer look."

He was familiar with her work? *Really?* She knew she had talent, of course, but this was the equivalent of a freelance magazine writer getting a call from the head of G.P. Putnam's Sons offering to buy a manuscript from her. She had the undignified urge to squeal with delight and spin in gleeful circles, but then she got suspicious. She shot Tony a questioning look, but his bland expression gave nothing away.

"Thank you," she replied. "It's great to meet—"

But Marcus's attention had already wandered, and he was heading off to study some of her paintings. "I'll just have a look around," he said vaguely, producing a pair of edgy black-rimmed glasses from a pocket and slipping them on.

O-kay, then.

That left her to greet Cooper, the surly one. She shored up her courage, praying he wouldn't kill her for saying hello.

"Hi," she said, extending her hand. "Thanks for coming."

It took him a minute to shake because he'd been distracted by something over her shoulder. Snapping to attention, he took her hand, said, "Pleasure," in an indifferent voice, and then looked past her again.

Bemused, Talia followed his line of sight to discover Gloria still working on packing boxes.

"And you are…?" Cooper asked Gloria.

"The sister," Gloria told him. "Ignore me."

With that, she finished taping a box closed, swung it around and headed to the studio's back room, giving Talia a suppressed smile and a wink as she went.

Cooper stared after her, a vague frown marring his brow. "Excuse me," he finally said to Talia, and then wandered off to join his brother as they studied the paintings.

Which left Talia semi-alone with Tony.

"What's going on?" she asked, not bothering to hide her open suspicion.

Shrugging, he took his time answering, and her nerves stretched accordingly. He had to know that she was freaking out and overwhelmed in the presence of a couple of men who could give her career a huge boost with little more than a snap of their fingers.

"We told you. We wanted to take a closer look at your work."

"Why? Slow week? Did you run out of Picassos and Monets to buy and sell?"

"Not exactly."

"What exactly, then?"

"A couple things. First, a wall in my Hamptons estate was damaged in the storm a few months ago."

"And you decided to come down here and share that news flash with me?"

"Not that news flash, no. This one—a huge mural depicting scenes from *The Odyssey* was destroyed. My mother, who was a Greek professor, commissioned that mural, and she loved it. Therefore, it means a lot to me, and I'd like it to be replaced."

Talia blinked, letting all that information sink in.

Oh, no.

Oh, no.

Freezing her poker face into place, she waited for the rest, although she already had the terrible feeling that this conversation was going to culminate in a *Godfather*-esque offer she couldn't refuse, no matter how much she knew she should refuse it.

"Is that so?" she murmured.

They seemed to be locked in an impromptu game

of chicken, each trying not to waver or show weakness first and undermine their own bargaining position.

He watched her with narrow-eyed interest for a beat or two, waiting for some further reaction, but she wouldn't give him the satisfaction. For reasons she couldn't identify, it felt crucially important never to reveal weakness of any kind to Tony. If she did, she feared he'd swallow her alive in a single gulp.

When she didn't say anything else, his lips curled with what looked like reluctant admiration, as though he'd realized that, like him, she was a player.

She tried to look bored, which was hard given the way her heart thudded with the strain of waiting.

"Additionally," he continued, now studying the tips of his neat fingernails as he crossed his ankles and leaned against the table, "we'd like to commission a mural for the lobby of Davies & Sons. The main building over on—"

"—Madison Avenue," she finished for him. Like she hadn't had her nose pressed to the sleek glass windows of the auction house millions of times, desperate for a glimpse of the artwork inside.

One heavy brow rose, mocking her. "You're familiar with it? Excellent. We thought that would be a great place to showcase an edgy new painter. We want something that'll make people stop and stare when they walk in the building. You feel me?"

Oh, she felt him, all right. She also couldn't breathe.

"We figure we could unveil the new lobby mural at our fiftieth-anniversary gala the week before Labor Day. The artist we choose will get a tremendous amount of exposure. Of course."

Of course. *Bastard.*

Finished dangling his rotten little carrot in front of her starving face, he looked up and straightened his posture. There was a glint in his eyes that looked suspiciously like amused triumph, but, to his credit, he didn't smirk.

"Know anyone who might be interested?" he wondered.

Interested? She was damn near frothing at the mouth.

It took everything she had to shrug and keep her face blank.

"I couldn't say," she lied.

"Really?" That quirked brow of his rose higher, and her fingers itched to rip it off his amused face and stomp it beneath her foot like a fuzzy caterpillar. "Why don't you think about it for a minute."

Oh, she was already thinking about a lot of things.

First of all, there was a silky and disconcerting note in his voice that glided across her skin like a feather's touch and made nerve endings zing to life all over her body. Second, she'd been so sure that her path for the foreseeable future was set. She'd made her list of priorities, with no room for last-minute deviations.

She'd been working too hard, she'd thought.

Life was short and she didn't want to miss a second of it, so she'd planned to get off the merry-go-round and travel while she could. Choose different, better goals than merely being a successful painter.

She wanted, in short, to *live.*

Third, her superlative deductive skills had led her to one inescapable conclusion: this mural commission was a gambit to get around what she'd told him yesterday. She'd lied and said she felt nothing romantic for him, he knew she was lying, and now he'd manufactured a reason to throw them together.

He was betting he could wear down her resistance if they spent more time together.

He was right.

"Talia?"

"Why are you doing this?" she asked, low.

Like magic, the intensity burning behind his brown eyes died out, and his expression became as bland as a bowl of infant rice cereal with milk.

"Doing what? Proposing something that could benefit both of us?"

"You don't really need me."

His lips tightened into a grim line. "Is that so?"

"You're trying to uproot my life, Tony."

"I'm merely making a business proposition to you."

"I've told you I'm planning to travel for a while."

"Then tell me no," he said flatly.

She opened her mouth. Nothing came out. She closed her mouth.

He watched her, unsmiling. This moment—this decision—had somehow become too important for petty things like winning or losing, and he seemed to take no pleasure in her struggle.

"Why me?" she asked finally. "There are a million other artists who'd be—"

He edged closer, more firmly into her space. There was something predatory about him now, threatening in a way that had nothing to do with her physical safety. It excited her almost as much as it—he—terrified her.

"Well, now you're raising an interesting point, Talia. This is a good offer. Lots of other artists would snap it up in a heartbeat. So why are you acting like I'm serving you a plate of nuclear waste?"

"You're not answering my question. Why me?"

"Why not you?"

"I don't want to work with you."

"Because…?"

Was he trying to force her to say it? Again? Well, fine. "Because we have different expectations about our—" her cheeks flushed "—relationship."

He frowned, looking baffled. "No, we don't."

"You're not serious."

"I am serious. I told you I had feelings for you, you said you don't have feelings for me, so that's it. We're friends only. End of story."

Standing there with him, close enough to see the sparks of black-and-gold in his brown eyes and feel the heat from his body, it didn't feel like the end of any story.

It felt as though their story was just beginning.

"So you've just…given up. Is that what you're telling me?"

"No means no, Talia," he said lightly. "You stood right there, looked me in the eye and told me you don't have romantic feelings for me. Remember that?"

As if she could forget. Even now, the lie clogged her throat, threatening to choke her. "I remember."

Though his expression was still unfathomably blank, his voice was the purest spun silk. "You're not a liar, are you?"

The funny thing was, she wasn't normally a liar, and the whopper she'd told yesterday felt as if it was scraping years off her life.

Could he see it on her face? The longing she felt for

him, locked in a death match with her fear of being hurt, her fear of being left, and all the other terrors that stalked her in the night? Could he feel the way her frustrated desire for him radiated off her skin like steam? Did he know that the thought of him was a relentless ache inside her, never giving her a moment's peace?

Did he know that she reread his letters all the time and kept them in a treasure box that held no other treasures?

"I never lie," she lied.

He hit her again with that lopsided smile, but this time there was something hard about it, almost cynical. Her belly responded by tightening into sickening knots.

"That's what I thought." Shoving his hands in his pockets, he shrugged. "So don't worry. I'll never mention it again."

The promise did nothing to improve her mood. "You won't?"

"Absolutely not. So are you interested?"

Having run through all her lies and accusations, she had precious few weapons left, so she tried bravado. "You couldn't afford me."

His eyes agleam with quiet satisfaction, he reached into an inner pocket and pulled out a folded check, which he held between his first two fingers the way he might hold a tip for a bellman.

Arrogant jackass.

Irritated beyond words, she snatched it away and—

Oh, my God.

She stared down at the check, stalling for time and making sure she hadn't miscounted the number of zeroes.

She hadn't.

How the hell was she supposed to walk away from this kind of a deal? she wondered with growing desperation.

She was a successful artist, true, but right here, in her hot little hands, she was holding more money—and opportunities—than she'd made on her last three commissions combined. Here she'd thought travel was her heart's desire. Hah. It turned out that she was, at the core, a ruthlessly ambitious artist who couldn't turn her back on the almighty dollar, the same as every other person in the universe. Besides, with this kind of money, she could buy her own small island in the Caribbean and spend winters there.

Even so, she didn't have to make it easy for him.

"Tony, I—"

He checked his watch, as though he was tired of her wasting his time and wanted to wrap up this whole annoying negotiation so he could get to the important part of his day.

"I'll give you the other half when you've finished both murals."

Dumbstruck, she stammered like an idiot. "The— the *other half?*"

"I assume that's okay?" he asked mildly.

Was it hot in here all of the sudden? Why did it feel like there was a tightening noose around her neck? What the hell had her greed led her into?

Increasing desperation made her fling out the only remaining excuse she could find. "Maybe your cousins don't think I'm the right artist for the lobby mural."

"Good point." Twisting at the waist, Tony looked to Marcus and Cooper, both of whom were bent over one of her paintings, murmuring and pointing. "So what do we think?" Tony called.

Marcus backed up a step, cocking his head to look at the painting from another angle. "She's got potential, but the work is still immature."

Ouch.

"So we don't want her for the lobby mural?" Tony asked.

Marcus moved closer to the painting again, squinting at her brushstrokes. "I didn't say that. In a couple of years, I expect she'll be getting six figures a pop. I'm seeing flashes of brilliance here."

Talia stilled, her queasiness fading as her insides launched into a happy dance. Brilliance? Did he say *brilliance?*

"I'm assuming she's qualified for a project this size…?" Marcus continued.

Tony shot her a questioning glance. "Are you qualified?"

Was she qualified? Screw him! "I have an MFA from Columbia."

"She's qualified," Tony informed them. "Coop?"

Cooper stood a couple of paintings down from his brother, studying a canvas so hard she was tempted to offer him a magnifying glass. He waved a hand. "I'm sure she'll be fine."

"I think that's everything," Tony said. "Do we have a deal?"

No. No, they did not have a deal. Things were moving much too quickly for her. What had happened to the quiet life she'd had a mere fifteen minutes ago? Why couldn't she shake the feeling that nothing would ever be the same after this?

"I'm not sure I should trust you," she blurted.

Tony stilled. "Let me make sure I understand what you're saying. You think that I'm so wild about you that I manufactured a reason to work with you, coughed up a ridiculous amount of money and dragged my cousins down here to meet you, all with less than twenty-four hours' notice? Is that right?"

This, naturally, made her feel like a narcissistic peacock, and her face flushed accordingly as she began the painful process of backtracking.

"Of course not. But I'm just not sure—"

"You know what?" Tony wheeled around and headed for the door, snapping his fingers and signaling for his cousins to follow. They did without a word, falling in line behind him. "This isn't going to work out. Sorry we wasted your time. Have a nice day."

Tony's hand was on the knob when something came over her.

Screw it. Fear already owned far too big a chunk of her life. She wasn't going to let it rob her of this once-in-a-lifetime opportunity, as well.

"Wait!" she called, the check pressed to her chest.

Tony paused but didn't deign to face her again.

"When do I start?" she asked.

"Today's Friday, so I think Monday is a good time. Have a bag packed so my driver can bring you out to the house tomorrow night. He'll pick you up at three. Oh, and he'll pick you up this afternoon for a visit to the auction house. You can get a feel for that mural, as well, but I want you to do the one at the house first."

"Wait, *what?*" Her brain slipped and slid, having so much trouble keeping up that she felt like a three-year-old struggling to ice skate for the first time. "A bag—?"

Tony's head came around, and the unmistakable gleam of triumph in his eyes made a hard lump of dread solidify in her stomach.

Another shoe was about to drop on her head—a big one.

"Oh, didn't I mention?" he asked. "You'll have to live on the estate for the duration of the project. Naturally."

"Wait a minute," she cried. "I didn't agree to—"

Tony wasn't listening. His attention had been irrevocably snagged by the new noise of nails clicking on the floor and jangling tags. Talia's belly dropped as though an elevator had fallen out from beneath her.

Not now, God, she prayed. *Not now.*

But God was apparently working on bigger projects at the moment, and didn't answer.

They all watched as a furry black-and-white paw batted open the door from the back room and Talia's border collie appeared, although she should've been asleep in her crate and therefore invisible, at least until Tony and his entourage left.

Damn canine.

Tony stared, riveted, as the dog trotted over to Talia and sat. After a long moment, Tony's gaze swung back to Talia, but it was sharper now. His gaze was knowing, as though he'd discovered that there was nothing she could hide from him that he wouldn't root out and discover.

"Border collie, eh?" he murmured casually.

"Yes," she admitted.

"What's her name?"

Talia hesitated, feeling her carefully crafted life and lies beginning to crumble. "Chesley," she told him.

Chapter 4

The Madison Avenue offices of Davies & Sons were, Talia discovered that afternoon, spectacular. The building was sleek and modern, a shimmering slab of gray glass rising above the surrounding buildings and pointing toward the sky. The minimalist atrium had a splashing fountain running down one wall, a huge spiral staircase that seemed to float up into the atmosphere, and boxy black furniture, each piece probably costing more that that check Tony had given her earlier.

The second she walked in and saw the bare wall beyond the receptionist's desk, she knew that Tony was right. This office and her work were MFEA—made for each other.

The ideas began to spark, making her manic with excitement and slowing down her steps as she walked through the double glass doors and up to the desk.

Luckily, the receptionist was on her game. "Talia Adams?"

Talia tore her gaze from her wall—yes, it was her wall now, and she was going to make it spectacular—and smiled. "Yes. I'm here to see—"

"Mr. Davies. I'll call him for you." The woman pushed a button on her phone and spoke to Tony through her headset. "He'll be right down," she told Talia.

"Thanks." Talia felt hot color rise up through her cheeks and wished she could tamp it down. Jeez. She was like a walking thermometer, shooting into the red zone every time Tony, or even the possibility of Tony, came up. How pathetic was that?

No wonder Tony accused her of sending mixed messages.

Hell, she was surprised he was hearing *Leave me alone* from her when her body was so full of *Take me, I'm yours.*

Get a grip, girl, she told herself sternly. *Focus on the mural.*

Easier said than done, but she did try.

The space was so stark and open. She liked that. Uncluttered, with only the bare necessities. So the mural would have to be equally spare, but vivid, which meant yellows and oranges. They weren't her favorite but maybe something like *Sol Splendor,* which she had, after all, painted for Tony, would be a good place to start. But she was also feeling a lot of green here, and that meant there was a lot of potential for—

"Talia," said a male voice behind her. "You're right on time."

Wait a minute, she thought, some of her excitement slipping. *That was the wrong voice.*

Turning, she discovered that it was the wrong Mr. Davies striding toward her with his hand extended— Marcus, not Tony.

Disappointment gave her a strong kick in the gut, but she ignored it and glued her smile in place as they shook hands. Since there was no possibility of she and Tony getting together, she refused to entertain the idea that she was disappointed to miss him.

Tony wasn't there to greet her? Good. So much the better.

"Good to see you again, Marcus. So this is the space, eh?"

"This is the space. What do you think?"

"I think I have a lot of ideas for this wall."

He grinned. "I figured you would. So has anyone given you the nickel history lesson yet?"

She already knew a bit—well, a lot—about the family's history, having checked Google before she came here, but she played dumb anyway in the hope of learning more.

"Nope. Hit me."

"Well, my father and his brother, Tony's father, founded the place fifty years ago. It wasn't on Madison Avenue back then, though. It was just a small house that did a good job with estate sales and jewelry collections and the like. We got our big break when a couple of big movie stars sold off their art collections. The rest is history."

He was being modest. "A couple of movie stars," she knew from her research, meant the 1960s equivalent of

Brad and Angelina. Still, she appreciated a little humility.

"And now you handle pretty much everything, right? Vintage cars, art, jewelry, wine, antiquities—"

"We hate to turn down a challenge. We've got departments and specialists who handle the auction end."

"And you're the president—"

"Yeah, but I don't want to mislead you. It takes the three of us to keep this ship running. I oversee day-to-day operations, Coop is in development and public relations, and Tony's going to replace our finance guy who retired last— Speak of the devil."

The elevator doors slid open and Tony stepped out, briefcase in hand and a harried frown across his forehead. He'd been heading for the glass doors to the street, but upon seeing them, he veered and strode over.

There was no time to prepare. Talia's skin experienced that slow sizzle of awareness that only Tony could cause.

The whole suit thing didn't help. There was something about seeing him—again—in that charcoal suit with white shirt and red tie that really did a number on her equilibrium. Good thing she'd never seen him in his army dress uniform. She'd probably crash to the floor in a dead faint.

"Where are you off to?" Marcus asked him.

"Meeting." He swung that brown crystal gaze around to her, kicking her heart rate up a couple of dizzying notches. "Do you like your wall, Talia?"

"I love it." Typically, her enthusiasm for an exciting new project came through in her voice, making her sound like a cheerleader in the middle of a round of rah-rah-rahs. "I can't wait to get started with the—"

Tony checked his watch.

Wow. Way to slash a woman's ego down to size. Talia's smile wobbled, but she somehow hung on to it. "I don't mean to keep you."

"Not at all," Tony replied, but he was already on the move again, slipping through the glass doors without a backward glance at her and only a quick wave for Marcus. "I'll catch you later."

"Yeah," she said lamely, fighting a ridiculous feeling of disappointment. "I'll see you—"

Too late. At the curb now, Tony raised a hand, hailed a yellow taxi and zoomed down the street, out of her line of sight.

"Why don't I give you a quick tour?" Marcus asked, gesturing her toward the elevator.

Talia stared after Tony.

"Talia?" The elevator dinged, and Marcus held it open for her. "Tour?"

"Sure," she said, her face burning with something she didn't want to identify.

The mansion was, in a word, unbelievable.

Really, Talia thought the following night, as the chauffeured town car rolled to a stop in front of Tony's Hamptons estate, she should have been prepared for it. Having consulted Google for everything she could discover about the Davies family and seen several online pictures, she knew that the house was in the English country style, with a shingled roof, lots of dormer windows and a couple football fields' worth of manicured land fronting the beach. She got all that. But getting it while seated in her own comfy home office in front of her computer screen, and getting it right here, right now, were two different things.

Part of the issue was that she'd never spent time in the Hamptons, that playground of the rich and famous, so she had little experience with this kind of property and wealth.

The bigger part of the issue was that she was still reeling from the unexpected turns her life had taken since Tony had shown up yesterday.

And of course, she'd be seeing him again in a minute.

A shiver of anticipation started deep inside her body and radiated out, skating across her skin.

Foolish, she told herself. She was being foolish with a capital *F.*

Not that there was anything she could do about it except ride it out.

A couple of deep breaths helped. By the time she'd gathered her purse and her courage, the driver was opening the door and holding out a hand for her, as though she'd be forever stuck in the car otherwise. Right. Because this was how rich folks rolled. So she accepted his silent help and climbed out, trying not to gape and stare.

She gaped and stared anyway.

The house had a circular drive, explosions of black-eyed Susans and manicured grass so green that it could have been ripped from a park in the Emerald City. There were also cobblestone paths, potted plants and mature trees providing shade at strategic intervals.

Talia had, in short, wandered into the pages of *Architectural Digest* magazine. If anything, she belonged in *Better Homes and Gardens.*

So, yeah. She'd have to fake it for a while. She could do that.

Resisting the urge to help the driver retrieve her luggage from the trunk, she strode to the front door, infusing her steps with a confidence that she did not remotely feel. Her efforts to look graceful were further damaged when her heel caught on one of the cobblestones, making her stumble. Arms pinwheeling, she recovered just in time to see a wheelchair-bound man emerge from the shadows inside the front door.

A young guy, he had a short and dark buzz cut, a bulky chest, immense and tattooed arms, and legs that were missing below the knee.

He was stifling a grin at her expense.

There was nothing she could do except laugh at herself. "Yeah. My nickname is Grace."

The guy's grin widened, and she decided that she liked him. "It'll be our little secret, sweet cakes," he assured her.

"I appreciate that." She extended her hand and it was immediately swallowed in his firm grip. "And I'm Talia Adams. Not sweet cakes."

"Oh, I know who you are, sweet cakes. Never you fear. I'm Michael Bianchi. Call me Mickey. I know everything around here. Just don't tell the boss that."

She laughed again. "Well, since you know everything around here, you probably know that I'm here to repaint the mural."

"Are you any good?"

"I'm the best," she said, with a rare burst of bravado.

"Modest, too. Hey, what's with that hair? Am I gonna need my sunglasses with you or what?"

She shrugged, smoothing the edges around her

temple. "I like colors. I'm an artist. What's with the tats?"

Mickey, who was wearing a short-sleeved shirt, had so many tattoos of varying colors running up and down his heavy arms that they might have been inked by Jackson Pollock. He didn't seem to mind the teasing. "Touché. I hope I'm not going to have any problems with you."

"I hope I don't have to give you an attitude adjustment. By the way, where's the accent from?"

"Where do you think?"

"I'm thinking somewhere in Jersey," she told him. "Probably near the shore."

"Ten points for the artist. Let's get you inside. Show you around a little bit."

With strong and efficient movements, he spun his chair around and led her through a foyer that was only slightly smaller than the lobby in Carnegie Hall. She saw a stately staircase, exquisite antiques and expensive rugs in every direction. It was, in short, one of those houses where an accidental twitch of the arm became thousands of dollars' worth of damage.

Given her occasional clumsiness, this was going to be quite the challenge.

Mickey gestured down one half of the hallway. "The kitchen is through there. We've also got a study, a den—"

"Hang on. What's the difference between a study and a den?"

"Lady, I've been trying to figure that out for years. The rich are different. Let's just leave it at that. Out back is the pool and then beyond that is the beach—"

All very lovely and interesting, but there was only one thing on her mind right now. "Where's the mural?"

"Upstairs. This way."

He led her to an alcove under the stairs, where a tiny elevator was hidden. A minute later, they were up on the second level, and the doors were sliding open to reveal the most beautiful mural she'd ever seen.

She stepped out, gasping.

The mural stretched along the hallway opposite several enormous windows that let in every possible beam of sunlight. The view included a stretch of lawn leading to the pool, which, in turn, led to a path through the dunes and to the beach on the other side. She could only imagine how powerful the storm's fury must have been to break these windows (they'd since been replaced) and damage the wall with water.

Even pockmarked and water stained, the mural was breathtaking, with vivid colors, meticulous strokes, and scenes that seemed to leap off the wall: Odysseus and the cyclops; Odysseus and the Sirens; Odysseus caught between Scylla and Charybdis.

"Oh, my God," she breathed.

"You got your work cut out for you, don't you?" Mickey asked cheerfully. "I hope you're up for the job."

More bravado kicked in, which was good because she had the feeling Mickey would eat her alive if she showed any signs of weakness. "Of course I'm up for the job."

He raised one brow. "You sure about that?"

"Yeah, I'm sure about that. So you can stop busting my chops."

He chuckled. "Well, what can I do you for? Do you want to get settled? Unpack?"

"I want to get started."

"Yeah, but—"

She stepped up to the wall, smoothing her hand over Odysseus's face, ideas flowing through her the way they always did at the beginning of a project.

"First I need to get this wall primed and repainted. Do you have supplies?"

He jerked his head toward a corner where, sure enough, there was a worktable loaded with cans of paint, primer, rolls, brushes, drop cloths and anything else she might possibly need.

"You just let me know if you need anything. The boss told me to put myself at your disposal."

At this mention of Tony, her heart skittered. "Where is he?"

Despite all her best efforts, there seemed to be a plaintive note in her voice, as though Tony had disappointed her by not being here as part of her welcome committee. Which was ridiculous.

Mickey's shrewd gaze narrowed. "He's not here. Why do you ask?"

"He might have some instructions for me."

"Like I said—if you need anything, I should get it for you." He shrugged. "I'm not even sure how much the boss will be here in the next couple of weeks."

"Oh?"

"Yeah. Oh."

Mickey waited, a wicked glint of amusement shining in his eyes.

Talia gritted her teeth. "And why's that?"

"He's got an auction house to run back in the city, doesn't he?"

Yeah, but she'd hoped—

Don't go there, Talia.

"And where's everyone else? Sandro, Skylar and his son—Nikolas, isn't it?"

"They took off for D.C. Sandro's starting a new job down at the Pentagon. They need to pick out a house, don't they?"

There went another tiny stab of disappointment. She'd hoped to meet Tony's family. "Oh."

The muffled bleat of a cell phone startled Mickey. Reaching inside a pocket on the side of his wheelchair, he pulled out his phone and hit a button.

"Yeah?" he barked.

Was it Tony? The mere possibility made Talia's idiotic heart race with excitement, which was irritating.

Maybe it was Tony. So what? Big deal.

Look at the mural, girl.

She did, trying to appear engrossed. Her eardrums, meanwhile, strained so hard for any remote sound of Tony's voice that it was a wonder they didn't rupture.

"Yeah," Mickey was saying. "Yeah. Okay. Sure. Okay. Got it."

She moved farther down the wall, studying another portion of the mural.

"Okay," Mickey concluded. "Later."

Working hard on her nonchalant act, which needed some serious practice, Talia turned back around, brows raised, in case it had been Tony and he had some message for her.

"So…"

"So. Where were we?" Mickey scratched his head. "Oh, yeah. Just let me know if you need anything. And no one expects you to start until Monday, so don't go working overtime. There's no bonus for trying to be the busiest beaver around."

"Good to know." She paused, losing the battle with her curiosity. "So, ah…any idea when Tony will be back?"

His eyes agleam with that annoying amusement—what the hell was so funny about a simple question?—Mickey held the phone up and waved it at her.

"Funny you should ask. That was him on the phone. He's on his way back." He winked, a wicked grin inching across his face. "If I'd known you were so interested in him, I would have told him just now. But don't worry, I'll be sure to mention it the next time I see him."

To her further aggravation, the death glare she shot his way only made him chuckle.

After a delicious dinner of fresh lobster, pasta salad and strawberry shortcake with Mickey in the kitchen—he turned out to be a great cook and even better company, keeping her laughing with stories from basic training and his tour in Afghanistan, where he'd served with Tony and Sandro—Talia went upstairs and organized her workstation near the mural. She lingered there for hours, telling herself that she was trying to get lost in the project, the way she always did, and that it had nothing to do with Tony's eventual arrival and wanting to see him.

Lies. All lies.

Still, she gave the busywork the old college try. She took pictures of the existing mural, studying it from every angle and imagining what she would change, and what she would keep the same. She set up the drop cloth and several spotlights, to make it easier to work late into the evening. She made preliminary sketches. She looked at colors. She studied books on mythology that she'd brought with her, seeking inspiration.

She waited for Tony.

At eleven twenty-eight, when Mickey had long retired to the caretaker's cottage and the house was dark and quiet, she heard the unmistakable roar of a car's engine outside. She froze, her body tight with anticipation.

Well, this was a problem. She had a choice. She could do the smart thing, which involved turning out the lights, gathering up her books and sketches, and tiptoeing down the hall to her bedroom, where she could escape before Tony ever came upstairs. Or she could do the self-destructive thing and wait for him.

The options were not equally matched. In fact, the idea of going to bed without seeing Tony first was the rough equivalent of visiting the Louvre for the food in the cafeteria without seeing the *Mona Lisa:* unthinkable.

Anyway, the decision was already out of her hands.

The front door opened and closed with a quiet click. His footsteps trailed off into the kitchen, where she heard the distant opening and closing of the refrigerator. Then he was back, striding up the stairs and appearing in front of her with all that masculine energy humming around him.

"Hi," she said, dropping one of her brushes on the floor and hastily snatching it up again.

"You made it."

"I made it." Feeling flustered and clumsy, as though she'd suddenly acquired an additional pair of hands and didn't know what to do with them, she grabbed one of the books she'd been perusing and held it. "You have a beautiful home."

"Thanks. Did Mickey feed you?"

"Very well. He's quite the character, by the way."

Tony unleashed that grin on her, making dimples bracket his cheeks and a slow curl of awareness tighten in her belly. "You have no idea." He looked over her progress thus far, frowning. "You're burning the midnight oil. I hope you don't think I'm that kind of a slave driver."

She shook her head. "I wanted to get started. I'm really excited—"

He nodded with no real interest, then took a step away from her, toward another wing of the house. Worse, he raised a hand to cover the beginnings of his yawn.

This rudeness, on top of his barely speaking to her at the auction house earlier, was starting to really tick her off. Which was absurd, because she'd told the man that their relationship was nothing special, and she really needed to stick to that position.

Still, her feelings were hurt. "Am I keeping you awake?"

"Sorry. It's been a long day. I'm off to bed."

So he was going then. Good. Great. That was for the best.

"Tony," she blurted.

He hesitated, looking back over his shoulder. "Yes?"

"I, ah, want to make sure you really want me to do this."

One dark brow quirked. "Do what?"

Once again, she floundered, and there wasn't a damn thing she could do about it. Something about receiving the full impact of all that intensity rendered her slow and half-witted. To add insult to injury, another bout of the clumsies hit her just then. For no particular reason, the book in her hand slipped, and she bobbled it to keep it from hitting the floor.

Did he really want her to stay here, in his house?

Did he really want to treat her with this cool indifference?

Did he really want to infect her mind the way he did?

Trapped, as usual, behind her fear, she asked none of those questions.

"The, ah, mural," she said. "Are you sure you want me to paint over it? A good conservationist could probably—"

His face closed off, telling her she'd have a better chance convincing him to hire a chimp with a box of crayons to work on his precious mural.

"I'm positive." His expression was dark and unreadable. "You're exactly the person I need."

Chapter 5

This plan of his, Tony privately conceded the next morning, might have a kink or two in it.

Which, given his attraction to Talia, shouldn't come as any major surprise. Still, it did. Or maybe his turmoil was simply a sign of how bad he had it for the woman.

Damn woman.

The plan was, of course, brilliant in its simplicity. He had lured Talia here, to his beautiful seaside home, with an offer he knew she as an artist couldn't refuse. They would get to know each other under the safe and nonthreatening (he hoped) pretext of working together. They would grow closer without him pressuring her in any way and he would give her the space she seemed to need. Their relationship would deepen over the course of the project, culminating in a romantic relationship that would include enthusiastic and, if he was lucky, frequent sex.

The end, right?

Not exactly.

For one thing, he hadn't factored in the difficulty of sleeping in the same house with Talia. The fact that she was under his roof, sleeping in one of his beds, within walking distance, was really doing a job on his mind.

Really ate away at him. Really made him crazy.

Then there was the whole giving-her-space thing, which was, let's face it, a hell of a lot easier said than done. Why did she need space? How much space was appropriate? What if he ate breakfast when she was eating breakfast? Was that a violation of the space rule?

Thus far, he thought he'd done an excellent job of giving her space.

Hadn't he let Marcus handle the whole auction house visit even though Tony had been dying to spend the time with her? Hadn't he hustled himself off to bed last night rather than linger, talking with her into the wee hours, which was what he wanted to do? Hadn't he feigned minimal interest in her?

Oh, yes, he had, and there was more.

Hadn't he let her eat breakfast alone in the dining room this morning? Hadn't he exiled himself to the weight room off his bedroom, pumping iron until his muscles burned? Hadn't he tried to ignore the scenery out his weight-room window, his spectacular view of the beach, including a spectacular view of Talia trying to paddleboard?

But he'd ended up watching her anyway.

She'd been a tiny figure against the sand, wearing a black string-bikini bottom and, unfortunately, a

black long-sleeved skin shirt. The ensemble also included a purple swim cap, which was perfect for her.
The distance was a problem, but he'd been able to see
the shapely length of her brown legs, the curve of her
hips and her exceptional heart-shaped ass.

A really great ass.

The image of her laughing and splashing in the
waves as she tried to get her balance and actually
paddle on the board further ate its way under his skin.
Talia was out there on his beach—with Chesley the dog,
by the way—having fun.

Without him.

But, hey, he was giving her space. That was part of
the plan.

Why was that part of the plan? He couldn't remember.

Anyway, he'd finished his weight lifting, come
down to the beach and was now ready to commence
the second part of his usual physical fitness routine,
which was a jog along the beach. And here was that
whole giving-her-space thing again, rising up to bite
him in the ass. Should he pretend he didn't see her over
there in the water? Just head on his way? Would that be
rude?

Could he manage it?

No. He really didn't think so.

From the first second he'd laid eyes on Talia, he'd
been unable to manage his attraction to her, which had
always been startling and undeniable. He remembered
the day he met her like it was ten minutes ago.

*That afternoon, as a favor to Sandro, who'd had a
conflicting meeting, Tony had swung by Talia's studio*

*to pick Nikolas up after his painting lesson. Arriving a
few minutes early, he knocked on the door and waited,
his mind full of the artists he'd been cataloguing at the
auction house—one-eared eccentrics with red hair, or,
alternatively dark-haired eccentrics with handlebar
mustaches and Spanish accents.*

*He hadn't expected the door to swing open and
reveal a laughing, gray-eyed woman who would change
his life.*

He froze, his hand still raised midknock.

*She was beautiful, with a dimpled smile and white
teeth, light brown skin and those sparkling eyes that
seemed to contain all the warmth and energy of the
sun. She was also decked out like a woman from ancient Athens, complete with white toga slung over one
bare shoulder, a white ceramic pot cradled in the crook
of an elbow and a wreath of green leaves perched atop
her cascading tumble of black curls. Her body was lush
with breasts and hips that curved to perfection.*

*His brain stalled out, and his thoughts fluttered
away like breeze-blown confetti.*

*She waited, brows on the rise, as though his drop-
jawed silence amused her.*

"I, ah," he began.

*"You weren't expecting a goddess to answer the
door?"*

*He heard the swell of repressed laughter in her
voice. "No. I was expecting Salvador Dali, to tell you
the truth."*

*She shrugged. "I don't paint like him, either. Sorry
to disappoint."*

*She was a lot of things, but a disappointment wasn't
one of them. "I'm not sure I have the right place."*

"I'm not, either. Who the heck are you?"

"Antonios Davies."

"What're you doing here?"

"I'm picking up Nikolas Davies. My nephew."

"Well, then you have the right place. You'd better come in."

She swung the door open, admitting him into a studio that was full of easels, paintings, light and the smell of turpentine. From a back room came the chatter of young voices and the splash of water.

"They're just getting cleaned up," she informed him, setting her pot on the nearest table and stretching across it to straighten up a couple of bins of paint tubes. Her round ass, he noticed, was a thing of beauty. "He should be out in a second."

"Great." Tony was engaged, and he hadn't so much as looked twice at a woman since he'd put that ring on Skylar's finger, but getting this woman's name suddenly seemed important. "Should I call you Helen of Troy, or...?"

"I prefer Athena, actually."

She laughed again, and the sound was so contagious that he found himself grinning at her and easing closer, as though he wanted to reach out and touch her joie de vivre. He wasn't normally a grinner, especially with complete strangers, but there was something elusive but significant about her that encouraged laughter and easy banter. If she gave him another thirty seconds, he'd probably be telling her the story of his life.

"Well, don't keep me in suspense. What's your name?"

"I'm Talia. I'm the artist and teacher. I'm also to-

*day's model, since the one I hired for the students didn't
show up."*

"Models," he muttered. "You can never trust them."

"That's a sad fact of life, isn't it?"

"So does Nik have any talent? Tell the truth."

"He's got a lot of talent. Wait'll you see his charcoal
sketch of me. You'll love it."

"We'll see."

"'We'll see'? I have a skeptic on my hands. Do you
doubt his talent, or my skill as a teacher?"

"No comment."

"And what do you know about art, pray tell? Do you
paint?"

"I appreciate. I studied art history in school."

"No way. Where'd you go?"

"West Point."

"Get outta here. There's no art at West Point."

"There is art at West Point," he assured her.

"So what do you do now?"

"I'm in the army."

For the first time, her smile dimmed. "What are you
doing roaming around with the general public, then?"

"I'm on leave. That's allowed."

"But—"

"I'm going back to Afghanistan next month."

That killed her smile outright but, to her credit, she
recaptured it pretty quickly. "Back? So you know how
to stay safe, right?"

"Let's hope so."

"How long will you be over there?"

He tried to keep his voice light, but that was hard
with the shadow of war doing its best to block out the
sun. "Not long. A year."

"I've never really met a soldier. I guess I don't travel in military circles."

"You've met one now, haven't you?"

"I'm going to write to you." She hesitated, seeming to think better of this plan. *"Or do you have too many pen pals already?"*

This announcement infused him with an unreasonable and inappropriate shot of happiness. Too late, he remembered Sky and felt a stab of guilt, which he shoved aside. It wasn't as if he was going to date this art teacher. A few letters while he was overseas. What could happen?

And honesty was always the best policy.

"Not many. Just my fiancée." It seemed important to get that out there, for the record. Or maybe he just needed to remind himself that this woman could never be anything more to him than a friend.

"Will she mind? Tell her I'm not trying to steal you away or anything. I have a boyfriend."

He stared at her.

For one bewildering second, before he caught himself, he tried to decide which possibility was worse: that she spent her nights rolling around in bed with some faceless but clearly lucky dude, or that she was oblivious to what he considered some pretty serious electricity crackling between them.

But, again—he was engaged.

This woman, and any other interesting woman who might happen across his path in life, was therefore off-limits.

On the other hand, he could always use a new pen pal.

"I don't think she'll mind," he told her.

"Great." Beaming, she grabbed pen and paper from the table and handed them to him. "I've never been a pen pal before. I'll be great. You'll see. I'll take my responsibilities very seriously."

He'd lapsed into grinning again—her smile was very contagious—but he paused to fix her with a stern look before he wrote down his information.

"See that you do. It's very bad manners to get a soldier's hopes up and then never write."

"I won't let you down."

Talia hadn't let him down, ever.

Until that terrible day when she'd rejected his final letter.

Why had she—

"What's up, Cap?"

"Hey, Mick," Tony said automatically, not fully registering Mickey's presence. "What's up?"

"Well, I was thinking about taking some lunch down to the beach."

The thing was, Tony reminded himself, Talia was afraid of something, and he needed to respect that. Give her time. See if she'd open up—

"Are you listening to me, Cap? 'Cause I get the feeling you're not listening to anything I'm saying."

—But what if she never opened up? What if she kept all those walls between them? What then? It wasn't as if these art projects were going to last forever—

"And I'm thinking that I could start babbling a bunch of nonsense right now and you'd never notice, Cap. For example, what if I said the Taliban is coming up the lane right now? What do you think? What about if I said this giant-ass meteor is heading right for our beach and we'll be dead in ten minutes? Would you hear me then? What if I said that I think that woman has your panties in a bunch? What about that?"

—And what if she finished both projects and they never came any closer than they were now? Huh? What then, genius? And what if—

"What about this, Cap? What if I say her name a few dozen times? I think I'll try that. Talia. Talia... Talia... Talia."

The name registered with Tony's frazzled brain.

With a fair amount of difficulty, he yanked his gaze away from where Talia was now tumbling off her paddleboard for the thirty-third time, and turned to face Mickey. The smartass was sitting there in his chair with a picnic basket in his lap, grinning up at him with that smug expression that could only mean he'd gotten the best of him. Again.

"Are you trying to be funny, Mick?"

Chuckling, Mickey ran a hand over his stubble. "I'd say I was being funny. Between you and your lovesick brother, I don't think there's a clear brain among the Davies men these days—you know what I'm saying?"

This assessment did nothing to sweeten Tony's mood. "I don't know what you're talking about, but I'm thinking of just ignoring it."

"And to think they put your sorry ass on the front in charge of a bunch of men," Mickey said sadly, shaking his head. "What's the army come to?"

"Yeah. Okay." Tony did a lunge or two, trying to look as though he'd been engrossed in his prejog stretches. "I'm doing my run. I leave you here to your nonsense. Maybe the seagulls need a laugh."

"Actually, Cap, I have a better idea. Why don't you

take this basket on down to the beach and have lunch with Talia? Since you'll be thinking about her anyway, you might as well give her a little face-to-face action."

Tony hesitated.

This proposal did have some appeal. He could run his ass up and down the beach until he dropped from exhaustion, or he could eat some of Mickey's excellent cooking—he'd recently taken some professional cooking classes and had taken over cooking duties at the house—in front of sparkling waves with his favorite person in the world.

Hmm. Tough choice.

And Mickey *had* given him the perfect excuse to break his rule about giving Talia space, hadn't he?

Tony shrugged, trying to look indifferent. "If you insist."

"Oh, I insist." Mickey handed the basket over. "I definitely insist."

Tony continued down the boardwalk, breathing in the salt air until it saturated his lungs. On days like this, he could almost forget that he'd ever left home. That he'd ever been to Afghanistan. That there'd ever been—and still was—a war.

Although, to be fair, was it the ocean setting that did it for him, or Talia?

Tough question.

Hitting the sand's edge, he toed off his running shoes and socks and slipped his feet into its giving warmth.

Something about her was brighter than other people. More intense, maybe. And it came across in person, but also in her letters. Maybe that was why he was so hung up on her. She was so…exuberant. So energetic and engaged.

Splashing around with Chesley now, she seemed infused with the sunlight, as though it came from inside her rather than from without. She and the barking dog were having fun, splashing, kicking up water, and Talia was laughing at nothing in particular. Even her silver toe ring shimmered against the bright water, and her bracelets, which she apparently never took off, tinkled like a thousand little bells.

He wanted…*that*. The weightlessness. The joy.

It seemed unlikely that he'd ever feel that kind of joy again, though; maybe the war had amputated it. Hell, the way he was wired these days, it was much more likely that the sunlight would hit him and immediately be sucked into a hole of black nothingness, never to return.

But he was working on it.

Wasn't knowing you had a problem and wanting to do better half the battle? God, he sure hoped so.

He'd reached Talia's umbrella and the pair of Adirondack chairs underneath, so he set the basket down and took a couple of steps toward her. She hadn't seen him yet, but was squealing with delight and turning away as Chesley did one of those crazy dog shakes, throwing water in every direction.

Raising a hand, he called to Talia. "Mickey sent me down here to—"

He froze, knowing something was wrong even before it happened.

Talia, still a good twenty or thirty feet away, grimaced, putting a hand to her chest and then moving it to her throat. She gasped in a breath, then another, but it didn't look as though she was getting enough air. His first wild thought was that she had choked on something, but she hadn't been eating—

Talia's mouth opened wider; her skin was beginning to pale.

"Talia," he called sharply.

Dismay widened her eyes. She held up a finger in a *wait a minute* gesture, not looking happy to see him, but that was just too damn bad. The adrenaline rush made him sprint flat out, and he reached her side just as she doubled up, bending at the waist and bracing her hands on her knees.

Since he didn't know what the hell else to do, he put a hand on her back to steady her and felt the straining heave of her rib cage. Panic tried to clamp down on him, but he shoved it away. Freaking out right now wouldn't help Talia, and he'd surrender himself back to the Taliban before he let anything happen to this woman on his watch.

"I'm—okay," she gasped. "Give me…a minute."

Okay? Did *okay* now mean that your face was chalky from lack of oxygen? Had she lost her mind?

"You're not okay. Sit down. Put your head between your knees."

She straightened, fixing him with a glare even as the tendons in her neck strained with each breath. "You… are way too…bossy."

"Damn straight. Here. Let's get you to a chair."

Keeping a firm hand around her waist, he steered her to one of the chairs where she sat, leaned back and closed her eyes. If he'd been a cat, he'd have lost eight and a half of his nine lives during the period that she breathed deep, in and out, slowly catching her breath, until it eventually returned to normal.

He waited, not wanting her to tire herself by answering any unnecessary questions, but then he couldn't take it anymore.

One of her hands rested on the arm of the chair, and he took it, squeezing. She squeezed back, and he let himself be reassured, at least until she opened her eyes. Evidently, she'd caught herself, because she looked embarrassed and, worse, uncomfortable with the caress.

She pulled her hand away and flashed what she evidently thought was a soothing smile.

"I'm fine. Don't worry."

"*Don't worry?* You serious right now?"

"Yeah, I'm serious. I just got a little overexcited and…lost my breath, and…it's no big deal. Don't you ever get overexcited sometimes? It's not like you need to call out the coast guard or anything."

Apparently they'd observed two different incidents, because that version of events didn't jibe with what he'd just seen. "That was a whole lot more than you just being out of breath," he said flatly. "Do you have asthma?"

"No."

"Pneumonia? A heart condition?"

"No. Just drop it, okay? I'm telling you…I'm fine."

"Fine," he snapped, running a hand over his nape and deciding to come at her from another angle. This woman gave *stubborn* a whole new meaning, and he was beginning to understand that trying to force her to do anything she didn't want to do was the rough equivalent of trying to fly without the benefit of wings or an airplane. "I'm not trying to make a federal case out of this, but you might want to think about seeing a doctor."

Uh-oh. Wrong tactic. So much for the calm and rational approach.

Reaching for her towel, she began drying her legs with the kind of jerky moves that told him she was pissed off, and royally so.

"I'm not an invalid. I don't need to see a doctor. And I'd appreciate it if you'd back off, okay? Back. Off."

"Talia—"

"Don't make me sic Chesley on you."

The dog, who'd been watching anxiously, whining, fixed Tony with a warning look. "Don't even think about it," he told the dog.

A sound vibrated inside Chesley's throat, and it sounded suspiciously like a growl. But then Tony snapped his fingers at her, she headed off toward the waves.

Stalemated, Tony and Talia glared at each other for a minute. It crossed his mind to just toss her over his shoulder and march her back up to the house, but he figured that would end badly for him.

Anyway, she was the one with the fearsome-looking dog.

He was overreacting, he supposed. If she said she was fine, then she was fine. God knew his instincts were all out of whack when it came to her.

"Fine. And when you collapse, I'll know what to tell the EMTs, won't I? I'll be sure to tell them I tried to get you checked out."

"Nice." The beginnings of a grin curled her lips. "Throw me under the bus, why don't you?"

"I will."

"What're you doing out here, anyway?"

"Well, I was jogging. I'm allowed to jog on my own beach, aren't I?"

Her lips thinned with obvious suspicion.

"But, as it happens, I ran into Mickey heading out with the picnic basket. So I thought I'd save him a trip and bring it instead. But since you're being so snippy, I think I'll take it back inside and eat it by myself."

Deciding to make it look good, he grabbed the basket and started for the boardwalk. That was all it took.

"Wait!" she called. "Let's not be too hasty. What's in the basket?"

"Do we have an agreement that you're going to be nicer to me in the future?"

"That depends on what's in the basket."

"Let's see." Coming back, he sat in the second chair and dug into the basket. "We've got your basic cheeses… I saw potato salad… Chocolate chip cookies… Oh, and—" He hesitated, not wanting to throw them back into uncomfortable territory. "It's, ah—"

"Let me see that." She snatched the bag in question from him and studied it, a flush rising up over her cheeks as she read the label. "Wasabi-covered peanuts."

She stilled, refusing to meet his gaze.

Yeah, Tony thought. *This was what you called an awkward silence.*

"Don't worry," he said quickly. "I won't force you to eat any."

To his overwhelming relief, she blinked and smiled up at him. It was one of those glorious smiles, bracketed by dimples and that sexy little mole at the corner of her mouth, the smile that he'd been living for these last months.

"You know—a good friend of mine loves these things," she told him. "I think I'll give them a try."

So, okay…lunch. Lunch would probably make sense. Yes. They should eat. Lunch.

If only she weren't so freaking flustered.

Talia fumbled through the picnic basket, arranging plates and cutlery and trying to pretend that Tony didn't exist. Failing that, she tried to pretend that he wasn't so…there.

Unfortunately, he seemed to be everywhere.

There was no safe place for her to look, at least none that she'd found so far. Another reach into the basket brushed her arm up against the sinewy warmth of his forearm.

"Sorry," she muttered, drawing back and concentrating on slicing a block of cheese instead. Although, given her general clumsiness and her current jitteriness, maybe she should leave the sharp objects alone. With her luck, she'd end up thumbless by the end of the meal.

She couldn't look him in the face, either, because connecting with that brown-eyed gaze was like plugging into a generator humming along at full power. A single second's contact was enough to heat her face to the melting point and make her brain liquefy.

The probability of making it through the entire lunch in some sort of dignified manner was, therefore, negligible at best.

Their chairs were way too close. They were arm to arm, and if she stretched her right leg out by a scant half inch, they'd be thigh to thigh, as well, and wouldn't that be more than her overwrought nerves could handle?

Still, it wouldn't hurt to take a peek. Just a quick one.

Under cover of swiping sand off her ankle, she bent and cast his legs a sidelong look, thoroughly checking him out.

Wow. That was all she could think. Just—*wow.*

He was sprawled in his chair with the relaxed posture that big men always used, as though it was their divine right to take up all the available space because their body mass was greater than anyone else's.

His nearest thigh, which was smoothly brown and sprinkled with a fine layer of black hair, was so sculpted and proportional it could have been snatched from a med student's anatomy book. His thigh was longer than hers, of course, and she didn't need to touch it to know that it was probably ten times as powerful. He had the toned calves usually seen on tennis players, swimmers or ballet dancers. Down at the end of all this lengthy perfection, his strong toes burrowed into the sifting sand, flexing and digging...flexing and digging.

His feet were big and—

Whoa. She didn't like where that thought was headed. Why didn't she just whip out a tape measure and be done with it?

He smelled good, too, which was a lesser problem, but still worth noting. What kind of man smelled good while exercising? What was so special about his skin, that he could generate that warm musk and cottony fresh scent when other men in the same situation would smell like barn animals?

How was it even possible that she could smell him over the salt water's tang?

That was the problem with Tony. He somehow managed to be everywhere while sitting quietly in his chair and minding his own business.

And she was the genius who'd agreed to come live in his house. With him.

Brilliant, Talia. You're a regular Einstein, aren't you?

Another wave of breathlessness hit her, and she tried to regulate the in-out of her lungs a little better, rather than struggle against it. The last thing she needed, or wanted, was for Tony to think she was an invalid just because—

"You okay?" He gave her another one of his searching once-overs, his arm suspended as he reached for the potato salad.

"Yes." That syllable sounded a lot surlier than she'd meant it to be, and he didn't look convinced, so she decided it wouldn't hurt to open up, just a little. "I overdid it. Okay?"

He stilled, those heavy brows sinking over his eyes.

Silence always made her babble, which was an unfortunate habit.

"I mean," she continued, shrugging and trying not to look directly at him as she indiscriminately loaded food on both their plates. Cheese. They needed more cheese. No, wait—they had enough cheese, but none of the crusty bread. They needed crusty bread. She reached for the bread knife, gesturing with it. "I just… I'd been out there in the water for a while, and before that, Chesley and I took a long walk on the beach, and before that, I didn't sleep that well, so it was all just—"

"Didn't sleep that well?" His gaze sharpened down to a needle's point. "What's wrong? Don't you like your room?"

"What's not to like? Staying in your house is like staying with Donald Trump, without all the tacky gilt."

The interrogation continued, gaining strength. "Is the mattress too hard?"

Her brain flashed back to that cottony slice of heaven. "No."

Tony stared at her and, honest to God, those amazing eyes—long lashed, warmly brown and sparked with gold—were like heat-seeking missiles because they gave her nowhere to hide.

"Then what kept you from sleeping?"

Thinking of you, down the hall. "Nothing. I mean… you know, it was just…new place and all that. New job."

"Right."

Was that it with the questions, then?

"So," she said.

"So."

The most uncomfortable seconds of her life passed.

"Well." Her voice was now hoarse, so she cleared it. "Cheers."

"Cheers."

Looking down at the plate on her lap, she discovered that she'd loaded it with three times as much food as she needed. Perfect. Now, she'd inevitably not finish it, which he'd point to as further evidence that she was under the weather.

Oh, would you get over yourself? she told herself sternly, reaching for a cracker.

They ate. Overhead, gulls flew. Waves splashed. Chesley ran down a crab, caught it in her mouth, and crushed it with great canine gusto. The sun shone. She and Tony chewed.

After several minutes, Tony spoke out of the side of his mouth.

"Wow. My lunches aren't usually this excruciating. I blame you."

That made her grin, and some of the tension between them eased back to a manageable level. "I beg your pardon. You pick a topic, and I will conversate intelligently with you."

"Conversate? Is that a word?"

"It is now."

"Okay. Here's my topic—are you excited about the mural?"

The mere mention of the project made her grin like a hyena. Undignified, maybe, but she couldn't help herself. "I'm thrilled. I can't wait to get started."

His gaze flickered between her eyes and her smile. "See?" he asked softly. "This is why I knew you'd be perfect."

"Don't get too excited. You may want to reserve judgment until you see my version of Odysseus. Maybe I'll give him green skin and blue hair."

Tony's smile flashed, boyish and white. "Like yours, you mean?"

"Bluer."

"Works for me."

He glanced up at the top of her head, where her purple swim cap was currently roasting her head like a baked potato in the oven, and her heart sank. Another pulse of self-consciousness hit her, and she smoothed the edges of the cap over her nape. Funny, wasn't it? Other women wore bathing suits to the beach and spent the whole time worrying about how their butts looked from behind.

With her, it was all about the hair.

To her relief, though, Tony didn't mention it.

"Okay," he said. "I have another question for you."

"No fair," she complained around a bite of cookie. "You're double-dipping."

He ignored this. "You said you wanted to travel more, right? Why's that?"

Startled, she paused to grab a napkin and dab at her mouth. Out of the frying pan and into the fire, apparently. She shrugged, trying not to make a big deal out of a simple question.

"The usual reasons, I suppose. Life's short. I work too hard. I should make more time for fun things."

He raised a brow and shot her another one of those skeptical sidelong glances. "I had the feeling there was more to it than that. You sounded like you were really making it a priority."

She studied her plate, ignoring the increasing burn in her cheeks. "Well, how do things ever get done if you don't make them a priority?"

"Good point."

"Anyway, you should travel, too."

His mouth twisted with so much bitterness it was a wonder she couldn't taste it. "I've spent enough time away for a while. I need to be home. Actually, I need to figure out how to be home. That would be a good start."

"Give it time," she said gently. "You're not Superman."

He looked back at the waves, his jaw hardening. "I got that lesson beat into me by the Taliban, thanks."

This was the first time he'd mentioned the suffering he must have endured, and she wasn't ready for it.

Fear congealed in her chest, weighing her down. Was she pathetic or what? He'd been the POW, and she was too terrified to even hear about what he'd gone through.

"Tony—"

She reached for his arm, meaning to comfort him, but his skin was hot to the touch. She jerked her hand away, burned by the thrumming urgency in his tight muscles, and then he looked at her again, right in the eyes.

Oh, God.

"You have to help me out here, Talia." His voice was a low rasp that connected more to her heart than it did to her ears. "Am I supposed to pretend you never wrote to me? Or that I don't remember what you said? Is that what you want?"

She'd never been much of a liar, but now would've been a great time to start.

Unfortunately, she couldn't manage it. "No."

His breath eased a little. "When you told me 'not today, Death'—that helped. It really helped."

Now, suddenly, *she* couldn't breathe—again—and it had nothing to do with overdoing it, not sleeping last night, or anything other than Tony's extraordinary effect on her.

"Did it?"

"More than you know."

"I'm glad."

"Are you?"

"More than you know."

They stared at each other, their gazes locked in place, and the magnitude of her mistake hit Talia all at once: she should never have come here to his home, where he was.

It seemed unlikely that she could spend any time with him—any time at all—without falling desperately in love.

Chapter 6

The sudden tension, which was pregnant and heavy, prickled across Talia's arms and up her nape, into her scalp. A breaking point hit them both simultaneously, and they blinked, turning away from each other. God knew what he was thinking; she couldn't think at all. She had another one of those painful moments of wondering why her fidgeting body couldn't sit still and what to do with her twitchy hands.

Tony, on the other hand, didn't move.

"So," she said after a beat or two, when the awfulness of the silence became more unbearable than the intimacy of that last topic, "maybe after lunch you can show me how to paddleboard before I drown myself—"

"The thing is," he said, keeping his face resolutely turned in the other direction, "if you have any more advice for me, now would be a good time to share it."

Was this a safer topic? It didn't feel safer, especially with his voice still in that husky range that twisted her up inside.

Lightening the mood with a joke or two probably wouldn't work, but what other defense mechanisms did she have available to stop this man from burrowing his way straight to her heart?

"Advice? I'm happy to offer an opinion on anything from your shoe selection to animal husbandry."

"Great. Then tell me how to get past the last several months."

"'Get past'?" she echoed faintly.

Just as she was beginning to feel grateful that he couldn't see her face while she wrestled with her unruly thoughts, he looked at her again, nailing her with an expression so lost and bleak that he might have been the sole survivor of the apocalypse.

"Yeah. I'd like to do some forgetting. I'd like to stop being afraid. I'd like to stop feeling like death is all around me, just waiting to pounce on me or someone who's important to me. What's your advice on that, Talia? How do I do it? How do I live a regular life? What if I never can?"

Never before had she felt like such an abject failure. Even her good friend sarcasm couldn't get her out of this one. "I don't know, Tony," she said helplessly.

"Give me something, Talia."

God. If only he knew what he was asking of her.

"Right now, all I can think of is this quote by Publilius Syrus—"

"The Roman writer?"

"Well, he was from Assyria originally, but yeah. He

said, 'I have often regretted my speech, never my silence.' So I should probably keep my mouth shut."

Tony snorted and shook his head. "Has he got anything else?"

"Yeah. 'Many receive advice, few profit by it.'"

His lips thinned. "This guy is batting zero with me, frankly."

"I warned you. I wanted to keep quiet, but no."

She hesitated, buying time and thinking hard. If he had any idea how uniquely unqualified she was to offer advice on the subject of living a normal and fear-free life, he'd probably bust a gut laughing.

Well, if she was in for a penny, she was in for a pound, right?

"He also said, 'The fear of death is more to be dreaded than death itself.'"

"Yeah," he muttered, "but I'm betting he was alive when he said it, so how the hell would he know? Maybe we should switch philosophers."

"Fine. I have one from that great sage, Charles M. Schultz."

"The writer of the Charlie Brown comic strip? Hit me."

"He said, 'I have a new philosophy. I'm only going to dread one day at a time.' But for you, I'd modify that to one hour at a time. How's that?"

Tony's brow contracted. His unfocused gaze drifted off again, toward the waves, and he mouthed *one hour at a time* to himself. Then he rested his elbows on his knees, and she got a quick glimpse of his scrunched face before he slowly lowered it into his hands. She watched, heart sinking, as his shoulders heaved.

Oh, no.

"Tony," she said, squeezing his forearm in a lame offer of support.

His head came up. To her surprise, there was a new light in his eyes now, and she went so far as to think he looked...relieved. Hopeful, even.

"One hour at a time," he repeated. "I can do that. I can get through one hour at a time."

"I know you can, Tony. I have complete faith in you."

"I don't know why you would, but...thanks."

"You're welcome."

"I don't know why I got on that topic. I just needed to tell you how much your letters meant to me, I guess."

Her mouth opened, and out came another of the mixed messages he'd accused her of sending his way. "They meant a lot to me, too."

It happened again. The air between them shifted and swirled, changing the mood during the time between heartbeats. In that fleeting second, they went from being friends to something dangerously and deliciously other.

She couldn't take her hand off his arm.

The intensity of the moment, like everything else in her life, scared her.

Their connection was more powerful than just the physical, but the physical weight of her hand on his muscular arm was so thrilling that she couldn't resist running her thumb over his skin.

His breath hissed—or was that hers?

"You know," he murmured, "you have a real knack for making things better and worse, all at the same time."

"I don't mean to," she said.

Even so, she damn sure couldn't stop touching him right now.

"Tell me." He leaned closer, bringing that heat and masculine urgency with him. "There's something important you're not telling me."

"No." That didn't sound convincing, so she tried again. *"No."*

"What are you hiding—"

Suddenly something invisible happened to him, and he stopped dead, flinching.

His eyes widened and fixed on a point behind her; his shoulders hunched in on themselves. Beneath her fingers, meanwhile, she felt the sudden stiffening of the muscles in his arm.

"Tony?"

Frozen to the spot, he didn't answer.

Alarm shot through her veins. Was he in pain? Having a heart attack? She glanced all around, looking for an explanation and someone who could call for help, because she'd stupidly forgotten her cell phone. But there was no one in sight and the coast guard chopper off the coastline was the only—

Inside her panicked brain, neurons began to fire.

Wait—was that it? The chopper?

"Tony," she cried.

His rigid body had begun to vibrate. If a marble statue could shake, she thought desperately, it would feel exactly like this. Following his line of sight, she saw what he saw: a clunky red coast guard helicopter sweeping the shoreline, buzzing close but not close enough to kick up the sand.

Tony was dripping sweat now. His black pupils were

so dilated she could hardly tell where they ended and his brown irises began.

Oh, God. Was this the fear he'd been talking about? Was this what life was like for him—everyday occurrences triggering debilitating panic attacks?

Well, she wasn't going to just sit here and—

"Tony." When he didn't answer, she clamped her palms on his jaws—delivering something like a quick slap. *"Tony!"*

His entire body jerked, including his gaze, which latched on to her face.

Was that progress? It sure didn't feel like it, not with his big frame still trembling from head to foot. She had a wild image of the industrial paint shaker at the hardware store. Had someone slipped one of those inside this poor man's body?

"Tony," she said again.

He blinked.

She smacked his cheeks again. Screw it. She could apologize later. She gave him another hard shake.

"Tony." Working really hard to keep her voice calm and her own growing panic at bay, she stared into his eyes. "Where are you?"

He blinked again then unstuck that throbbing jaw of his and opened and closed his mouth.

"You're scaring me, Antonios. You answer me, goddammit. *Answer me.*"

"At—at home," he said, his body now straining with the effort of drawing breath. "And I told you…not to call me…Antonios."

Something made her choke. She was either laughing or stifling a sob—she couldn't tell which. "Where is home?" she demanded.

"Sagaponack."

The helicopter, which had to be the slowest moving aircraft since the Wright Brothers flew their plane, made its meandering way out of sight, its rotors still audible for what seemed like ten minutes after it was gone.

But Tony was doing better. Maybe.

"Who am I?"

Another blink, and it was as though he slammed back into his body.

One second he was checked out, probably on some horrible road in Afghanistan under fire from the Taliban and receiving air support from U.S. helicopters, and the next he was present, focused and, judging from the color now flooding his cheeks, embarrassed.

"Talia," he said, wrenching free.

By the time she thought to tell him to sit still and recover for a minute, he'd already lurched to his unsteady feet. He staggered, which probably wasn't good for his humiliation factor.

"Jesus," he muttered, grabbing the umbrella pole for support.

"Here." She got up, too, reaching for him. "Let me—"

That was the wrong thing to do. He flung his arms wide, breaking free. "I don't need your help," he roared, his features contorted and unrecognizable with fury. "You think I want your pity? Huh? You think I want you to see me like this?"

God. This man was ripping her heart out.

"It doesn't matter, Tony—"

"Doesn't matter?" Some ugly sound came out of his

mouth. A laugh, maybe, or a verbal sneer. "I'm crazy, and it doesn't matter?"

"You're not—"

He stalked several feet toward the boardwalk, thought better of it and wheeled back around. "Is that why you don't want any part of me? Because you know how screwed up I am up here?" For emphasis, he jabbed two fingers at his temple.

God.

This man was going to shred her heart into mince-meat before this was all over.

"I don't think you're screwed up."

His lips peeled back, revealing teeth that seemed sharper than usual, almost feral. "You should," he said grimly.

"Tony—"

"So much for your advice, eh? I thought I could get through an hour at a time. Maybe I should break it down a little more. Maybe second to second is more my speed. I think that's about all I can handle. Don't you?"

"No, Tony—"

He stalked off, leaving only Chesley and the seagulls to hear her calling after him.

That night, Talia startled awake, knowing something was wrong long before she could pinpoint what it was. She sat up and blinked into the darkness, trying to get her bearings.

Her alarm clock's digital display read 3:21. Her room, like the house, was utterly silent, but for the distant white noise of the surf. Since she kept her drapes open to enjoy the spectacular view, there was enough moonlight dappled from the waves to show that nothing was out of place in her room. There were no looming shadows behind the chair in the reading corner, for example, and no figures darting out from behind the entertainment armoire.

And yet something—maybe everything—was wrong.

Had she had a nightmare?

Rubbing her eyes, she tried to shake off the anxiety—

Wait. What was Chesley doing?

The dog was sitting by the closed door, looking over her shoulder at Talia. When she caught Talia's eye, she whined and pawed at the knob.

Silly dog. Why couldn't she do her peeing at a decent hour, like everyone else did?

Muttering, Talia tugged a long-sleeved T-shirt on over her tank top and shorts, found her flip-flops, tightened her silky sleeping scarf around her head and was on her way to the door when she heard a muffled sound that made her spine melt.

It was the long, eerie wail of someone in pain.

Sudden fear rooted her feet to the floor. She'd never heard a sound like that, and whatever caused it wasn't good. The keening rose up again, drowning out the roar of blood in her ears, and the last of her sleep-induced confusion dissipated.

Tony. That was *Tony* in trouble.

Over at the door, meanwhile, Chesley was running out of patience. Wriggling with agitation, she gave a sharp bark easily translated into English: *hurry up, dummy!*

Talia snapped into action, throwing the door open

and heading down the hallway at a dead run. Guided only by a small console lamp and Chesley's haunches as she raced past, Talia sprinted around a corner and into another wing that she'd never visited, and then—

Oh, no.

This new corridor had a hundred freaking doors marching up and down its length, all of them shut. Which one was—

Chesley went straight to a door midway down, sat and barked at her.

Oh, thank God for this wonderful dog.

They were just in time, too, because Tony was going berserk now. The last of his wails twisted into something coherent. A desperate plea for help and for…her?

"Please. Don't do that! Don't— Talia… Taliaaaa… *Talia!*"

Without thinking about the wisdom of what she was doing, she banged through his door, ready to face any enemy that presented itself, armed only with her bare hands and her primitive desire to protect Tony from whatever had him.

Except a sweeping glance of his bedroom, which was even bigger than hers, revealed nothing. No raging fire. No bad guys. Not even Tony, because his massive bed was neat and empty.

What the—?

Once again, Chesley saved the day. Guided by that wonderful sixth sense that dogs have, she zeroed in on one end of the sofa, which was, Talia realized, pulled away from the wall at an odd angle.

Was Tony behind there?

The only answer was the sudden appearance of a

flailing arm on the floor behind the sofa and Tony's renewed yells.

"Talia! Taliaaaa—"

"I'm here." Ignoring all rules about letting dreamers sleep, or waking dreamers gently or whatever the hell you were supposed to do, Talia skirted the side table, knelt at his head and grabbed his biceps to calm him. He was faceup and shirtless, with his eyes closed and his arms overhead. Down at the other end of his long body, his bare legs bent and kicked, as though he needed to swim away from a monster or risk drowning. "Wake up, baby. I'm here. I'm here."

He struggled against his demons, twisting and writhing into the nest of blankets he'd made for himself back there, and then, quite suddenly, his eyes opened and he stilled.

He stared up at her, panting.

She waited. Though she had only a dark and upside-down view of him, she could tell there was no dawning recognition in his expression. Nor was there any lessening of the tension that had strung his body tight. If anything, he seemed poised to strike—

Beside her, Chesley whined.

A warning, as it turned out.

Tony struck with the lightning reflexes of a pouncing cheetah, lashing out and clamping down on her wrists. Even then, her sole thought was for his safety, not hers, and some inner peace took charge, filling her up and calming her down. There was only one thing he needed to hear, so she said it in a voice as soothing as she could make it.

"It's me, Tony. Talia. Everything's okay. It's me. I'm here."

The manacle grip of his fingers never loosened, even as he flipped over on his belly and did a military crawl out of the narrow space. He crept closer, looming over her where she knelt.

"It's me, Tony," she kept murmuring. "It's me."

Was he awake now?

Surely not. The light in his eyes was so ferocious—so intent—that it seemed dangerous to look directly at him, like eyeballing a full solar eclipse.

And yet she didn't dare turn away.

Finally she wound herself down, or maybe she ran out of air to breathe and therefore had none left for speaking. All she knew was that the world did a bewildering flip-flop, and she was no longer the one with all the answers.

Hell. Maybe she was the one dreaming.

"Tony?"

Instead of answering, he rose to his feet with the steady grace of Mikhail Baryshnikov, pulling her along with him. Naturally, she wobbled. The only thing standing between her and a face-first dive for the floor was the solidity of his grip, so she didn't pull away.

If anything, she leaned closer, studying him as he studied her.

The new silence was so profound that she'd swear she heard every blink of his eye and drop of sweat as it rolled down his brow. Certainly she heard every intake of his harsh breath, and every outward whoosh.

Or was that her breath?

Without warning, he released her wrists. This freedom from the scorching heat of his body should have been a relief. It wasn't. Those big hands of his went straight to her face, cradling it in a rough grip and angling it so he could see her better in the dim light.

"Talia?" His voice was gravel mixed with rock salt. "Is it you?"

"Yes," she breathed.

"You're here?"

"Yes."

The answers didn't ease him. If anything, the humming tension in his body rose higher, into a level beyond danger.

"Are you leaving me now?" he demanded.

The answer she wanted to give—the lie—wasn't the one that came out of her mouth. "No."

His searching gaze swept her face one last time, just to be sure, and then he apparently decided to believe her. One side of his mouth twitched, forming a dimple in his hard jaw.

There was no other warning before he yanked her into his arms, holding her tight.

Chapter 7

Tony's body felt good against hers.

Dizzyingly good. Too good.

He was big and strong, for one thing. Warm, with the clean scent of someone who'd showered just before bed. With her cheek pressed against the hard slab of his chest muscles, and her hands sliding up the bare satin of his back, it occurred to her, too late, that while he may have just experienced a moment of weakness, he was still the sexiest and most powerful man she knew.

And his body felt really good against hers.

Now that the immediate crisis had passed, she had time to focus on a few details that had escaped her attention until now. He was nearly nude, for one thing, with only a pair of low-slung boxer briefs covering him and, with their hips pressed fully against each other, she was in a position to note that it wasn't much cover.

He wasn't aroused, but he was well-endowed, and because she'd been celibate since Paul had ignominiously dumped her a while back, she noticed.

He held her tight, with hot puffs of his breath fanning her neck. There was no room to arch away, or to lock her arms in place so that her braless breasts didn't have to rub up against him. Their thighs were also pressed together, creating yet more points of electrical contact between them, and she had the insistent urge to hook one of her legs around his waist and thrust—

"Sorry." Pushing her away, Tony robbed her of that incredible sensory overload, leaving her body cold and her heart leaden. He walked to the window and stared out, running his hands over his head. "I'm okay now."

That was good, because she wasn't okay. Not at all. Maybe it was the forced intimacy of being clinched next to him in the middle of the night, or maybe her defenses were at a natural low because she'd been sleeping.

Or maybe those were excuses.

Maybe her need for him was just getting harder to control. The fact that she'd managed her feelings this long was, as far as she was concerned, a feat worthy of some kind of gold medal.

Bottom line? She didn't want to let him go.

"You sure you're okay?"

He kept his back to her, probably because he was embarrassed again. "Yeah."

There it was: her cue to leave and let this man process his demons by himself.

She ignored it.

"Can I get you some water or something?"

"No. Thanks."

Great. Everything was fine, and he didn't want her

help. It stung a little, but so be it. Her own wishes didn't matter at a moment like this, even if her hands itched to smooth over his back again, offering comfort. Even if she did want to sit on the sofa, take his head in her lap and massage his temples until the tension left his body. Even if her luxurious room did feel like a Siberian gulag compared to being here with him.

She hesitated, torn.

Chesley, who'd been watching the proceedings from a few feet away, trotted over and sat at her feet, waiting for her marching orders.

Talia snapped her fingers and pointed to Tony. Clearly the best dog in the world, Chesley headed straight for Tony and nudged his leg. This pulled Tony out of his dark thoughts long enough to look down at the dog and scratch her ears.

"Hey, pooch," he murmured. "How're you doing? How're you doing?"

Deep inside her chest, Talia felt some of her torment begin to ease. "Tony," she began.

"Go back to bed. I'm fine. I didn't mean to scare you."

Again, she ignored him. "Does this happen often? The night terrors?"

Those broad shoulders shrugged.

"Every night?"

Another shrug.

Okay. So he wasn't in the mood to talk. *Pick up on a clue, why don't you, Talia?*

But…he'd been calling her name.

"What was the dream about?"

"You don't want to know," he said, his voice hard now.

Was that a warning? It sure sounded like one.

"Actually," she said quietly, "I do want to know."

He wheeled around, facing her. The darkness shadowed his expression and made his eyes glint with something disquieting and equally irresistible.

"Go to bed, Talia."

He had a way of saying her name sometimes, turning the syllables into a velvety seduction that awakened nerve endings and made her yearn for things that weren't hers to have. Not in this lifetime. The warning note was there again, and she had to admire his sense of honor. They were heading in a direction tonight where they didn't need to go. Really, she should turn and walk out.

Too bad she couldn't.

"You said my name," she reminded him.

Was that a trick of the light, or did his sensual lips curl? "So?"

"You didn't call for your brother or your sister, or even your ex-fiancée. You called for me."

He said nothing.

"That seems important."

He took a step toward her. "So did your letters, but look how wrong I was about that."

There it was. The lie. She'd known it wouldn't take long to get there.

The ice was cracking beneath her feet, threatening to break, and yet she took a step closer. Did that make her a self-destructive fool?

Then she was a fool.

"You dream about me?"

"Does that surprise you?"

"Yes," she admitted.

"Why? Didn't we cover this ground already, when I came to your studio and you spit in my face?"

"I didn't spit in your face."

"No? What else should I call it when you lie to me and think that I'm stupid enough to believe it, beautiful Talia? A love letter?"

There was no answer for that, but her silence only infuriated him.

Another aggressive step brought him right up to her face, where he loomed, killing her with the anger in his glare.

"Huh?" he demanded, sweeping his arms wide. It was funny—the more unglued he became, the more certain she felt that she was walking the right path tonight, even though it scared her. "Do you think I don't see the way you look at me? Do you think I didn't notice you named your dog after my unit's dog in Afghanistan? Do you think I missed that little detail?"

"You have a lot of questions for me, don't you? But why don't you answer my question, Tony?"

"Why would I do that?" he roared. "Why would I tell you how I feel about you *again?* So you can look at me with those big eyes and feel sorry for me? Or maybe you're dying to tell me how you'd give the same comfort to any passing soldier who had a nightmare? Why are you screwing with my head?"

God. That was a sucker punch directly to her solar plexus. She wavered, fighting sudden hot tears, because she knew he was right, and the truth was ugly.

"I don't mean to."

"It doesn't matter whether you mean to or not. You *are.* And don't you dare stand there and cry on me."

"Fine." Blinking furiously, she swiped away her tears before they fell. "How about I tell you the truth?"

"That would be a refreshing change."

She took a deep breath. When that didn't help, she took another one. He waited, watching her every blink. As usual, there was something about his intensity that paralyzed her, making her feel clumsy and inadequate. All she could think was that if he hated the sight of pity in her eyes, it would kill her to ever see it in his.

Finally, he took mercy on her.

Reaching out, he took her hand and reeled her in, infusing her with some of his warmth and strength and loosening up her throat. She twined her fingers with his and held on, squeezing until she expected to hear the snap of several of their bones. Ducking his head, he pressed his cheek to hers and whispered in her ear.

"Tell me, baby."

"It's been a tough year."

Against her temple, she felt the prickle of his brow as it contracted, and she could understand his confusion. Maybe he thought she was referring to her broken relationship with Paul, which would be a natural conclusion. The wrong one, but still natural. Tony had only seen the tip of her iceberg of secrets.

She couldn't bear the though of telling him about the rest.

"I understand," he murmured. "I know about tough years."

"I'm strong. I can handle almost anything."

"I know you can."

"The one thing I can't handle," she said, raising her head so she could look him in the eyes, even though she was about one second away from bawling like a baby, "is having you and then losing you."

A glimmer of something—relief? Hope?—flashed across his face. "You're not going to lose me."

That did it. The first tear fell, splashing down her face. "It's inevitable."

His brow furrowed into a vague frown, but he chose not to pursue it now, which was, she knew, a temporary reprieve.

Instead, he lowered his head and, taking all the time in the world, covered her mouth with his.

Questions buzzed inside Tony's mind, demanding answers.

What was driving Talia's fear?

How could he convince her to trust him?

It was too soon, wasn't it?

Would she regret everything in the morning?

The second their mouths connected, though, all his questions evaporated into mist.

The first kiss was sweetly perfect, a gentle brush of lips so that they could get past the initial shock of intimacy and learn the feel of each other.

A catalyst, nothing more.

The next kiss was an explosion of all the things he'd kept too deep inside for too long and now could no longer contain.

He'd wanted her for too long. Needed her too much.

And now she was here. His.

This was no time for gentle exploration.

He just couldn't manage it.

"Talia."

Yanking away her scarf—why did women always

wear scarves at night?—he tunneled his fingers into her silky short curls, surprised at how close-cropped they were, and angled her head the way he needed it. There. Greed made him trigger-happy, but she drove him to it, sighing and opening for him so he could thrust his tongue deep, nipping, sucking and licking until it seemed possible—hell, likely—that he'd swallow her whole.

And then she surged up, digging her sharp little nails into his nape as she writhed against him and hooked one of her legs around his waist. Instinct made him clamp his hands on her ass (Jesus; it was firm and plump—perfectly round) and pump his hips, searching for the sweet cleft between her thighs.

"Ah, Tony," she gasped, her face twisting as her head fell back. "Don't stop."

That was it, then. The spot that made her unravel.

He thrust again, harder. "There?"

The only response was her sharp cry, followed by the thrilling sound of her breath hitching and then stopping.

She nimbly hooked her other leg around him, climbing him as if she was shinnying up a coconut tree.

Mindless now, he swung her around and headed for the bed.

There were things he should be saying at a moment like this, things she needed to know.

That her smile made his heart stop, for example, and that she filled his soul.

That he'd loved her almost since he'd met her, and always would.

That being with her was his blessing for having survived the war.

Did she know that? He'd have to tell her one day, when he could talk again and his need wasn't so urgent.

Ripping the linens back, he eased her down, laying her head on the pillow. Tears trickled from the corners of her sparkling eyes, but her lips, swollen now, were curled in a sensual smile that was sexier than he could've dreamed. Even that mole at the corner of her mouth was hot. He'd had other plans for her, but that mouth deserved a little more time and attention. So he settled his weight onto her pliant body, rocked his hips into the yielding cradle between her thighs and kissed her.

She cooed and murmured indistinct words, licking her way deep into his mouth, arching against him and scratching her nails up his back in one long stroke, and it still wasn't enough.

He held her velvety face between his hands, gorging on her eager lips and tongue, marveling at all the ways they could lick and nip each other—up and down, back and forth, thrusting and retreating—and he knew it could never be enough.

But he would happily die trying to get there.

He was hugely erect, so hard with wanting her that it was a wonder his straining member could contain the rush of blood. How many muscles did the human body have? Could they all snap at the same time? His were stretched taut, strung with tension, so it seemed like a distinct possibility.

Breaking the kiss, he rested his forehead against hers while he gathered the strength and restraint to stop touching her long enough to grab a condom from the nightstand drawer.

"I need you," he panted.

"I know."

"Now."

"Hurry," she said.

But she didn't make it easy for him. She'd planted one of her feet on the mattress—he caught a glimmer of that toe ring—and was using the leverage to rotate her hips against him. Her thrusts were rhythmic and insistent enough to make his vision dim with pleasure. Forget the condoms for now. Reaching up under her, he palmed her ass and held those flexing globes in his hands.

Magic.

Except that her little shorts were in his way, and he couldn't have that, now, could he?

So he worked his fingers under the elastic waistband, stripping shorts and skimpy panties down her legs in one fell swoop.

There she was. His prize—the last and only one he'd ever want. Waxed and bare, the thick folds ruddy and engorged. Glistening. He dipped his head, and she obligingly spread her thighs so he could smell her. She had that raw musk, the earthy fragrance of an aroused woman, and the scent, in combination with the lush fruity scent that was purely Talia went straight to his head in an intoxicating rush.

He licked her, needing a taste.

Her responsive cry was sharp and unabashed, and hot enough to drive him over the edge into insanity if he didn't get inside her *now.*

No, but wait—condoms.

Cursing with impatience, he levered up over her body, reaching for that drawer again, where he kept some ancient condoms from before his last stint overseas. Hopefully they hadn't disintegrated into rubber bits by now.

He was in luck. By the time he'd ripped the package open and peeled one out with his fumbling fingers, she'd taken care of his boxer briefs, yanking them down far enough for his erection to spring free.

He covered up, managing a shaky laugh. "I'm dying here."

She laughed, too, swiping at her sparkling eyes. "So am I. You have no idea."

Smoothing her forehead, he kissed it as he lowered his hips down into position. "So why are you crying?"

"Because I've wanted this."

That wasn't *quite* what he needed to hear. "Wanted…?" he prompted.

"You. I've wanted you."

He took his penis in hand and ran the swollen head back and forth between her folds, gasping at the slick heat.

"Since when have you wanted me?"

Another shimmering tear fell and, Jesus, he'd swear she melted as he eased inside her tight body, sighing and crooning as her eyes rolled closed. Watching her… feeling her…possessing her…it was all he could do to control his body's shudders as he tried to master a rhythm rather than fall into the frenzied thrusting that his surging blood demanded.

"Always," she said as their bodies began to rise and fall together, and her silver bracelets clinked in time to their movements. "I've always wanted you."

At that point, talking became impossible. Everything became impossible except his frantic effort to get close enough to her and to hang on to her once she splintered in his arms, calling his name and demanding more…harder…*now,* as she gripped his ass and took everything he had.

When he came, his body convulsed and he felt his face twist with ecstasy. He cried out, throwing back his head and letting loose with a hoarse shout that was full of joy, triumph and perfection.

It wasn't that he was perfect, God knew, and the haunted shadows behind Talia's eyes that she refused to share with him also made her less than perfect. They had issues, and he knew it—issues individually and as a couple. The thing was, though, they were perfect together. Perfect for each other.

Which worried him, because his life, thus far, had certainly not been a model of calm seas and smooth sailing. Anxiety niggled at him for as long as he let it, which was about two seconds. And then he shoved it in its dungeon, extinguished the torches and turned the key in its lock.

Later for that. Maybe never.

There…that was better. He felt lighter already.

Being with Talia felt like opening the door on a whole new world of possibilities. As though he was finally moving out of the black-and-white portion of his life and into high-def color. As though he could finally get out from under death's shadow.

Exhausted and emotionally spent, far beyond managing anything as complex as a smile, he stared down at her, wanting to make sure she was okay. Her brown eyes were wide and clear now, warm and intent. There were things he wanted to tell her, but now with their bodies and gazes connected, he had the feeling that she'd already seen and accepted everything about him.

"Talia," he began anyway.

"Shh." Sliding her hands up his shoulders and around his neck, she pressed him back down, took his full weight, anchored her legs around his and flipped the linens over them both. "We'll talk in the morning."

Wrapped up warm and tight, with his love in his arms, Tony lowered his head and fell into a peaceful, dreamless sleep.

Chapter 8

Talia didn't sleep.

She watched Tony, which was much more interesting. He was a starfish, hogging the entire bed with his arms and legs spread wide, and he seemed to spend equal amounts of time on his back and stomach. He didn't snore, nor did he seem to dream, although he did murmur her name once. In sleep, his face was smooth and relaxed, and it was possible to believe that he'd never been to war or suffered.

But what had he told her? The war always comes back?

Yeah. That.

She'd been fighting her own war this past year, hadn't she? In the morning, that fight would be back. Again.

So she didn't sleep.

When the first streaks of orange light crept around the edges of the drapes, she got up and tiptoed out of the room, trying not to disturb him. He didn't move, poor baby. God knew when he'd last slept well.

After a quick shower back in her room, she threw on a white tank and button-down shirt, a pair of khaki shorts and her electric-blue wig.

Blue was appropriate, she thought. No doubt she'd be ending the day in the depths of despair, so why not dress the part? Hell, she might as well put on a little Miles Davis while she was at it; *Kind of Blue* pretty much covered it.

Wow. Wasn't she the queen of self-pity this lovely morning?

Nice job, Talia. You're a regular role model to women everywhere, aren't you?

Well, it was time to get started on the mural. If nothing else, she'd been hired to do a job, and it was now first thing Monday morning, so she might as well hit the clock and get to work.

Okay, she though, surveying her work area. Where had she put her sketches? Were they back in the—

"Hey."

Oh, God.

Tony came around the corner from the other wing, stretching and smiling a sleepy, sexy morning smile. Apparently modesty was not a virtue he struggled with, because he hadn't bothered throwing on any clothes. His boxer briefs—they were gray, she saw in the morning light—were slung low over his notched hips, and there was an interesting bulge in front.

Her body tightened accordingly, which was ridiculous. Last night, she'd had the most amazing sex of her life and she really should be satisfied for a while.

She wasn't, though.

Tony crept closer, all gleaming skin, rippling muscles and sinew. But something in her face must have troubled him, because his steps slowed and he stopped short without touching her.

He stared at her, growing wariness in his brown eyes. "You're up early."

"Yeah. I couldn't sleep."

"I slept great." His dimples emerged, color flooding his sharp cheekbones. "You probably noticed."

"I'm glad."

"So am I." His voice dropped, becoming husky and seductive. "Come back to bed. I was really looking forward to waking up with you."

"Tony—"

His shoulders stiffened, squaring off, and a shadow darkened his expression. She hated doing this to him.

Hated everything about what would happen next.

"Don't do this to me, Talia. Not after last night. Don't push me away."

"I'm not. But…we need to talk."

Reaching out, he stroked those gentle fingers over her forehead, tracing an eyebrow…the bridge of her nose…the curve of her bottom lip.

"I don't want to talk. I want to make love."

"So do I," she admitted.

"Then what's stopping us?"

She swallowed, working hard to master the growing lump in her throat. "I've put this off long enough."

Behind them, the elevator dinged and the doors slid open. Mickey rolled out, already speaking in midsen-

tence. "I just thought I'd swing by and make sure—
Hey! Whoa! How about you two giving a guy some
warning?"

Talia wasn't up for facing Mickey just yet, but Tony
spared him a quick glance, waving a hand.

"Give us a minute, Mick," he said quietly.

"Happy to," Mickey muttered, backing into the waiting elevator again and punching the buttons five or six
times. "Anytime you're marching around in your Skiv-
vies, you can include me out."

The door slid shut again, leaving them alone in the
heavy silence.

Somber now, Tony hit her with that intense gaze of
his, so earnest she could almost hear the snap of her
heart as it broke in two. "We'll deal with it. Whatever
it is—it can't be that bad."

If only that were true. She couldn't speak.

"Talia? You're scaring me right now. It's not that bad,
right? You're not married, are you?"

Married. That would be so much simpler. "No."

"In hiding? An escaped criminal? Is that it?"

Talia opened her mouth, forcing each word out, because she knew that each syllable was a nail in the
coffin of their fledgling relationship.

"I—I've…had some health issues."

He nodded grimly. "I knew it. I'm going to get you
checked out—"

God, this was hard.

She shook her head. "I already know what's wrong."

Now he was the one who couldn't seem to get the
words out.

"What…is it?"

Just say it, Talia. "I have Hodgkin's lymphoma."

Tony went utterly still, all expression draining out of his face. She stared into his eyes, but he no longer seemed to be there, inside his body.

"Hodgkin's—?" he echoed softly.

"—Lymphoma. They used to call it Hodgkin's disease. Cancer, Tony. I have cancer."

Tony backed up a step, leaning into the wall for support. The color leached away from his skin, giving him a greenish tinge. "You have—"

"Cancer."

Blinking hard now, nostrils flaring, he fought a mighty internal war of some sort and seemed to master his emotions. He swallowed, and when he spoke again, his voice was firmer.

"What, ah…where are you with your, ah, treatment?"

"I've had chemotherapy. Radiation. And surgery."

His brows contracted. "Surgery?"

Without a word, she unbuttoned her shirt, revealing the puckered scar that ran between her collarbones.

She knew how it looked, but seeing the dawning comprehension on his face made it a million times worse.

"Jesus," he whispered. "How did I miss that last night?"

"We were busy with other body parts last night, weren't we?"

The joke did nothing to lighten the mood.

"So when you stopped writing to me—?" Tony wondered. "And all your dark paintings?"

"Right. I'd just been diagnosed. I didn't know what was going to happen, and I didn't think it was fair to encourage you when I was still seeing Paul."

The mention of the name did something to Tony, and

a bucketload of what might have been anger replaced the glazed look in his eyes.

"Paul?"

"He said that he loved me and he could handle anything." Bitterness made her voice harder than she would have liked. "And he hung in there, too. Up until my hair started falling out."

Reaching up, she pulled off her wig, deciding that she might as well hit him with everything at once. It was a relief, actually. The air felt cool against her scalp, and her hair was beginning to grow back. But it was taking forever, and she only had a scant half inch of silky curls at the moment.

And of course he'd had his hands on her head last night.

"I don't care about your hair," Tony told her.

Ah. Funny. Where had she heard that before?

Still, Tony was a different man from Paul. Maybe Tony actually thought he meant it. Maybe he did mean it.

His mouth worked, producing no sounds. He was so busy editing his words that he couldn't get anything out. She couldn't blame him. The process of dumping a sick woman could be pretty tricky, as she knew from painful experience.

"What's, ah, what's the doctor saying?"

That almost got a smile out of her. Really, he should've been a diplomat. He had the chops for it.

"What's my prognosis? I don't really know at the moment. I'm going to have another round of tests and scans soon. I'll know better then."

Tony's face contorted, but she felt the hurt. His

pained expression exactly matched what she was feeling in the center of her scarred chest.

"Why didn't you tell me?"

That made her laugh. "I did tell you. I told you I didn't have room in my life for—"

"Why didn't you tell me you were sick?" he roared.

"Why? So I could see you look at me exactly the way you're doing? With pity for the poor sick woman who's probably going to die soon? Are you serious?"

"Don't say that," he cried.

"Why not? It's what you're thinking, isn't it?"

He backed up a step. *"Don't ever say that again."*

She shrugged, suddenly too exhausted to speak.

It didn't matter.

Another backward step took him farther away from her, as though he needed to get out of her radius of contagion.

"I'm going to need some time with this," he told her.

Wow. Could she predict the future with eerie accuracy or what?

"Of course you are," she said bitterly, turning her back on him and resuming the search for her sketches.

Tony's only warning that an invasion was imminent was the jangle of keys in the lock of the penthouse's front door. And then the door swung open.

It was his sister, Arianna.

A visit from her was the last thing he needed at the end of this hellish week, when he'd retreated to the city to work at the auction house and get his mind wrapped around Talia's illness.

"Tony!" Opening her arms to him, she smiled with

such extreme delight that the guilt threatened to suffocate him. "Oh, my God! It's so good to see you!"

"Hey." Working fast, he rearranged his features into something approximating a smile and caught her just as she flung herself at him and wrapped him up so tight he had to wonder if she'd grown an extra arm or two. "What, ah—what're you doing here?"

Letting go of his torso long enough for him to gasp in a breath, she planted her palms on either side of his face and smothered him with kisses.

"You knew we were coming!"

"Was that today?"

Arianna pulled back, eyes aglow with happy tears. Motherhood really did agree with her. She was still pleasantly plump from her pregnancy but, if anything, it increased her beauty. There was a peaceful serenity about her that was so powerful it almost kept her feet from touching the floor.

"Yes, it was today." She squinted, giving him a critical once-over. "You don't look happy. What gives?"

Tony floundered around for an excuse. He was happy enough to see her, he supposed, but it would be better if she'd ease up, just a little. She had a real mother-hen thing going, and he could do without the incessant coddling just now.

He'd seen her back in Cincinnati already, right after the baby was born, and she'd tested the limits of his sanity with all the hovering and worrying. It was a blessing to be back from the "dead," of course, and a double blessing to be back with a sister who loved him so much, but—

"I just need a little space." He kept it gentle and to the point, hoping she'd understand. "I'm trying to get my bearings, and I don't need you fussing around me all the time, so I—"

"That's why we won't be here long," she sang, in what she evidently believed was a reassuring tone. "Just a couple weeks or so."

A *couple*—?

"Great," he muttered.

Arianna completely missed his lack of enthusiasm. She was patting his face again, smoothing her thumbs over the hollowed spaces under his eyes. "You're still too thin. I need to work on fattening you up a little. If I don't, who will?"

Irritated, he shrugged away from her clutching hands. He'd been eating just fine, and when you'd spent time as a POW, you were allowed to look haunted and gaunt for a while.

"I don't need—" he began.

"Excuse me," said a sarcastic male voice from the hallway, "but can you siblings suspend the bickering long enough for me to come into the house?"

Startled, they stepped back to allow Arianna's husband, Joshua Bishop, over the threshold. He gave Tony a grim nod as he passed.

Yeah. Tony didn't much like him, either.

For one thing, Joshua had served time in prison. He'd been freed through one of those innocence programs, true, but prison was prison, and God only knew what kinds of things he'd learned from the real felons in the joint.

Second, he was bulging with, as far as Tony was concerned, a thuggish amount of muscle and had a tattoo of some Adinkra design on his neck. His *neck*. Tony's tattoos, of tigers' eyes and dragons, on the other hand, were much more tasteful and were limited to his arms and torso. Where tattoos belonged.

Third, Joshua had an attitude that could best be described as...guarded. Moody. Surly. Suspicious. He was loving enough with Arianna, true, but with everyone else he was reserved to the point of being sullen.

Suffering from bouts of moodiness himself, Tony didn't have the patience for those traits in anyone else. So, yeah, he didn't like the cat.

Still, Joshua was a real estate tycoon who'd made something of his life since he'd been sprung from the big house, and Tony could respect that. In fact, that gave Joshua something in common with Tony, who'd also suffered a setback or two in his recent history and was trying to rebuild his life.

Most important, Joshua was married to his sister, and since Arianna clearly adored him and the horse he rode in on, Tony was trying to find the good in his brother-in-law.

Right now, for instance, Joshua was weighed down with two large duffels, one slung over each shoulder, and was also carrying Apollonia, the baby.

Yeah. The family was big into Greek names, which came from having a matriarch who'd been a Greek professor.

Apollonia was just a tiny little thing, had a Mohawk strip of black curls down the middle of her lolling head. She was fast asleep for the moment, strapped into a sling across Joshua's chest.

Seeing her, Tony felt the pull of something...primal.

She was a pretty baby, with sweet pink skin and a pouty rosebud mouth. Tony loved his little niece. He leaned down to smooth his hand over her downy soft spot and kiss her forehead.

"Hey, little girl," he cooed.

Joshua stiffened. "Have you washed your hands, man? You need to wash your hands before you handle a baby."

Straightening, Tony glared at his brother-in-law, who scowled back.

"So what's wrong?" Arianna demanded.

"Nothing. Why do you keep asking?"

This was, of course, an unnecessary question. He'd been just a notch or two above catatonic for the last several days, ever since making love with Talia and then being flattened by her bombshell, and he knew he looked pretty bad. Additionally, he'd never been particularly good at hiding his feelings from his sister, so she was probably reading him like a child's bedtime story right about now.

Hell, he had no idea why he was even going through the motions of denying there was a problem, except that he didn't want to spill his guts in front of her husband, the tattooed wonder.

"Something's wrong with you," Arianna insisted. "Spill. Now."

Joshua, who by now had almost tiptoed his way out of the room, patted the baby on the bottom with one hand and jerked a thumb in some vague direction over his shoulder with the other. "I'll just—"

Arianna looked around at him and beckoned him back with a wave of her hand.

Judging by Joshua's stricken expression, he would rather have been summoned for a laser eyeball peel.

"Why don't you stick around, honey?" Arianna

asked him. "You always have good advice. Maybe you can help Tony."

"Oh, I don't think—" Tony and Joshua began together.

Arianna naturally ignored both of them. "Sit down. Both of you."

With that, she marched off to the sofa and sat. After a fair amount of awkward shuffling and darting looks at each other, Tony and Joshua followed Arianna and sat on either side of her. Joshua took a moment or two to arrange the sleeping baby across his lap, which gave Tony time to get his thoughts together. But soon they were both looking at him with expectant gazes—actually, Arianna's gaze was expectant; Joshua's was pained, if not outright gloomy.

"Well?" Arianna asked encouragingly. "This is about Talia, right?"

Joshua stirred. "Talia? Who's Talia?"

"The artist Tony's in love with," Arianna said softly, out of the corner of her mouth.

A stab of alarm made Tony sit up straighter. "I never said—"

Arianna waved that hand again. "Whatever. What happened?"

He hesitated, trying to form the words around his twisting mouth. The words didn't want to come out. "She's…got cancer."

It was hard to say whose eyes opened wider, Arianna's or Joshua's. For the first time, Tony had a taste of what it must be like for Talia every time she told someone she'd been sick.

"Cancer?" Arianna echoed faintly.

"Hodgkin's lymphoma," Tony clarified.

They sat in silence, letting the words sink in.

"Oh, Tony," Arianna said. Her eyes filled with tears, and they fell down her pretty cheeks, making the conversation a million times worse.

"For God's sake, Arianna." Resting his elbows on his knees, Tony hung his head and tried to keep it together. "You're killing me here."

"I know," Arianna said. "I'm trying to stop. See? I'm stopping. Right now."

With a silent eye roll in his direction, Joshua plucked a tissue from the side table, passed it to Arianna and rubbed her shoulders. "It's okay, baby," he said in a soothing voice. "But you need to pull it together. Tony needs us to be strong right now."

Tony felt his brows inch higher with surprise. If anything, he'd expected Joshua to punch him in the mouth for speaking that way to Arianna, but apparently the brother could be an ally when he wanted. Good deal.

"You're right. You're right. I'm going to stop crying." Ducking her head, Arianna sobbed harder, pressing the tissue to her mouth.

Joshua chose his words carefully. "Arianna's had a...rough time with her...emotions, since the baby was born," he explained.

Arianna's head came up. "Why are you trying to sugarcoat it?" she snapped. "I have a little postpartum depression. It's perfectly normal. A little moodiness. The occasional mood swing—"

Joshua's brows rose toward his hairline, but he said nothing.

"—And a little moodiness. Big deal. But why do we have to tiptoe around it? I'm doing better, aren't I?"

This time, Tony thought he caught a glimmer of a smile in Joshua's glance at him.

"Yep. You're doing much better, baby. The medication is really working for you. I can tell a huge difference."

This seemed to perk Arianna up. With a final sniffle, she blew her nose, pocketed the tissue and turned back to Tony. "So what are you going to do?" she demanded crisply.

"Do?" Tony asked stupidly.

"Yes, do, you big oaf," Arianna snapped. "What. Are. You. Going. To. Do?"

Joshua's hand ran over Arianna's shoulders again, taking some of the fire out of her eyes. "If I know anything about your brother, baby," he said carefully, his steady gaze resting on Tony, "he believes there's nothing more important than being with the person you love and supporting them. No matter what. Isn't that right, Tony?"

Joshua and Arianna stared at him, waiting.

Was that what they thought?

"Of course I'm going to be with Talia," he told them. "I'm just praying I have the strength to do what she needs when she needs me."

Talia decided early that Friday evening, as she flopped onto her bed and wallowed in the familiar downy softness of her Navajo-patterned comforter and mountain of pillows, that it was great to be back in her own apartment, even if it was only for a weekend break from all the hard work she'd been doing on the mural.

Not that she'd been out in the Hamptons for that long, or that they'd mistreated her. If anything, her time at Tony's house had been like a luxury retreat from reality, with five-star accommodations, all the gourmet food Mickey could cook up for her, and that spectacular oceanfront setting, which made her seriously wonder how she'd survived so long in her landlocked little two-bedroom apartment.

It was just that she needed the soothing comfort of home right now, with the pale gray walls that she'd painted herself, her sandalwood-scented candles burning on the dresser, Chesley lounging in the corner chair with her paws draped over the arm, and Gloria.

Every now and then, she really needed her sister.

Even if Gloria did tend to get on most—if not all—of Talia's nerves.

Turning her head, she looked across the bedroom to her walk-in closet where Gloria was rummaging through clothes and probably making a royal mess. The continual scrape of hangers and the opening and closing of shoe boxes didn't sound encouraging, but what could she do? Talia and Gloria were the same size, and it was every sister's solemn duty to share her clothes when emergencies arose.

"Hey, Glo?" she called.

Gloria, looking hassled, with a strand of hair hanging in her face and several of Talia's expensive silk scarves draped across her neck, poked her head around the door.

"Yeah?"

"Thanks for coming with me this morning."

They'd been through this drill a million times before, so Talia knew what to expect…and here it came.

Gloria lowered her brows, making the familiar frowny face. "Don't thank me. That's what I'm here for. Did you think I'd let you go to the doctor by your-self?"

Talia flipped over onto her side so she could see Gloria better, resting her head on her palm. "No. But I'm not sure you know how much it means to me."

They didn't normally do emotions, she and Gloria, so it was no surprise when Gloria *tsk*ed and waved a dismissive hand. "Oh, you'll make it up to me, honey. When I turn up with breast cancer or Alzheimer's, I plan to be a much bigger pain in the ass than you are now."

That got a laugh out of Talia. "I look forward to it."

Gloria's gaze sharpened, running over Talia's face in one of her critical assessments. "You doing okay? You look tired."

"I'm fine." Talia had a strict policy that had carried her through her treatments: never acknowledge or give in to the periodic physical weakness. Better to drop into a dead faint from exhaustion than to admit that her body wasn't firing on all cylinders all the time, just like everyone else's. "Stop asking."

Talia caught a quick glance of narrowed eyes and pursed lips before Gloria ducked back inside the closet. "Stop being such a freaking martyr and take a nap," she called. "I won't tell anyone."

Talia dropped her arm and sank her head into her fa-vorite pillow, giving herself five minutes—no more!—to rest her eyes before she thought about dinner.

"I'm not a martyr. I prefer to think of myself as Wonder Woman. Or Buffy. I can handle anything."

A muffled snort came from the closet. "I stand cor-rected, O invincible one. So…what's going on with you and Tony? And please give me credit for putting my nosiness on the back burner all day. Are you impressed?"

"You know what would really impress me?" Talia called back. "If you went a whole day without being nosy. Why don't you shoot for that?"

"You don't want to talk about it? Is that what I'm getting?"

Talia hesitated. The thing was, she did want to talk about it. Sort of. The lead weight of her heartache was getting to be too much for her, and it might be time to share it.

Anyway, how could she feel any worse?

"I told Tony about the cancer."

There was a long silence, and then Gloria reappeared, eyes wide. "Hold up. Go back to the beginning. Are you telling me there's something going on with you and Tony? I was just fishing."

Talia glared. Why did they have to waste time on every little detail before they got to the main point of the conversation? "Get real. You saw him, didn't you? And he's a great guy. How could I resist that combination? Of course there's something going on."

Gloria hissed with outrage. "Well, why'd you have to act like I was insane for asking?"

Feeling unaccountably irritable, Talia shrugged. "I'm not happy about it."

"Because…?"

"Because when I told him I'd been sick, he said he needed some time to—"

"Well, give the brother a minute, Talia. It's a lot to take in."

Astonishment made Talia hike herself up into a sitting position so she could see her sister better. Notwithstanding her policy of endless second chances for the bastard she was dating, Gloria wasn't big on giving people the benefit of the doubt, especially men.

"What gives?" Talia asked. "I'm surprised you don't want to stake him through the heart."

"Illness scares people, Tally." Gloria's expression and tone were gentle enough to make Talia want to reach for a tissue. "They don't know what to do or what to say. It's like they get paralyzed. And anyway…"

She trailed off, blinking.

"Anyway," Talia prompted when the silence went on too long.

Gloria ducked her head, but not before Talia caught a glimpse of a tear as it trailed down her cheek. After a quick swipe at her eyes, Gloria shot her a rueful smile.

"Anyway," Gloria said, "I'd trade places and be sick for you if I could, no matter how big a pain in the ass you are." She paused. "Maybe he feels the same way."

"Aww." Talia squirmed and made an exaggerated pout to hide her discomfort. A close corollary to her rule about never admitting weakness was her rule about never showing emotion. Breaking either rule would quickly lead to the ugly cry, and once she started that, she feared she'd never stop. "I love you, too, Glo."

Gloria, luckily, was on board the *keep it cool* train.

"Yeah, whatever," she said, disappearing back inside the closet. "Enough about you. Back to me. What should I wear? Too bad I'm so much more petite than you. Your clothes always hang on me like a tent."

"Child, please." Grinning, Talia flopped back onto the pillow. "You'd be lucky to fit one of your cellulite-riddled thunder thighs inside anything of mine." They both laughed, probably because they'd worn the same size in everything since they were teenagers. "I don't know why you think you're going to find something in there," Talia continued. "You know I don't have any black or white clothes. You'll have to go with a color. Doesn't that make your skin break out in hives?"

"I told you. I want something colorful tonight. Aaron's taking me to Masa. He knows how much I love Japanese."

Right, Talia thought sourly, glad Glo couldn't see her roll her eyes. Aaron the married man was taking Gloria to a Manhattan restaurant.

Sure.

And the director of the Louvre was on the phone right now, offering to devote a section near the *Mona Lisa* to Talia's work.

It was really hard, but she bit back her words of warning and kept her mouth shut. Why risk getting her head bitten off again? It wasn't as if Gloria welcomed the truth, no matter how obvious it was. God alone knew no good had ever come from telling Gloria her honest opinion about the wonderful Aaron, so why would today be any different?

"And can you make me up?" Gloria called. "You do the liquid eyeliner so much better than I do."

"Sure," Talia said.

If she heard the lack of enthusiasm in her voice, Gloria gave no sign of it as she peered around the door again, holding up Talia's red vintage wrap dress. "What about this one? Do you think Aaron will like it?"

Oh, who the hell cared what that lying and cheating SOB liked or didn't like?

Talia stared into her sister's face, which was so eager and hopeful it was like watching a puppy in the second before it got kicked, and tried to dial back her frustration and confusion. Gloria was smart, funny and beautiful. What had happened to make her self-esteem so low that she was grateful for whatever crumbs a married man might drop her way?

Why wouldn't—or couldn't—she see the light?

On the other hand who was Talia to wonder about any woman's ability to see the light? It wasn't as if she was batting a thousand with her stellar selection of first Paul and then Tony, now, was it?

"That one'll make your butt look huge, Glo," Talia reassured her. "He'll love it."

"Perfect. Now for some shoes—"

Chesley's head came up off her paws and she cocked her ears. She jumped off the chair and trotted through the apartment and to the front door, just as the bell rang.

"Do you want me to—" Gloria began.

"I'll get it."

"Great. I'm going to change."

Gloria went to work unbuttoning her blouse and shut the closet door, leaving Talia to haul her tired butt off the bed and follow the dog, who was now sitting on her haunches and looking back at her with a lot of *hurry up* in her eyes. If there was any question about what she wanted, she gave a low *woof* and a follow-up whine as she pointed her snout at the knob.

"Will you hold your horses?" Talia muttered. "Give me a chance to check the peephole—oh, my God."

It was Tony.

Chapter 9

"Hey." Tony hovered in the doorway, clearly testing the waters and deciding what sort of reception he was likely to get before he came any closer.

Meanwhile, Chesley, a very poor judge of character, trotted over to him and nudged his hand for the obligatory ear scratch. Stupid dog. Didn't she know he'd let them down? Didn't she know a severe punishment was in order for the torture he'd put them through this past week?

Evidently not.

"Hey," Talia said.

"Can I, ah—can I come in?"

She shrugged and let him pass. Since her jackhammering heart was now lodged in her throat, it seemed like a good idea to keep words to a minimum.

"Sure."

She led him into the living room. At a gesture from her, he sat on one end of the sofa. She sat on the other. She waited. Nothing happened.

"How are you?" he asked after several of the most excruciating seconds of her life.

"I'm great. How are you?"

"Great."

They were both liars. She hadn't slept since Monday's painful parting scene, and it was all she could do to keep from drooping with exhaustion. He, in turn, looked like shit, with those haunted hollows under his eyes again, deeper than ever, and several days of bristle darkening his chin.

If he hadn't slept, either, it was no less than he deserved. Not that she was bitter or anything.

"I'm sorry," he told her.

"Don't be." Though she thought she had her anger under control, there was an unfortunate bite in her voice that she couldn't seem to dial back.

"I think I have plenty to be sorry about."

"Don't worry about it. It's all good."

Desperate for something to do with her hands, Talia began straightening her coffee-table books. Though she wasn't looking directly at him, she was able to see that his shoulders stiffened and his head shifted, as though he wanted to cock his ear and make sure he was hearing correctly.

"It's all good?"

"Absolutely." Her skittering nerves collided with her innate tendency to babble, and that, along with her desperate need to change the subject, made for an unfortunate combination. "Did you check out the mural yesterday? I really think Odysseus is coming along, don't you? I want him to look fierce and focused, and I'm also trying to bring out a little bit of his fear, but I'm just not sure—"

"Don't we have more important things to talk about than the mural?"

The growing incredulity in his tone went a long way toward soothing her hurt feelings. Not that she was ready to get past them yet.

"The mural is the only thing we have to talk about, Tony."

A low growl was the only warning before Tony lashed out, grabbing hold of her wrist and lowering it away from the books. Ignoring her sharp cry of surprise, he got in her face, his eyes a blaze of brown with gold sparks.

"I think we need to talk about our relationship. Where we go from here."

"There is no relationship. You made that pretty clear the other day. And if it wasn't clear when you walked out, it's been clear in the days since. You didn't call or text," she reminded him. "Either of those would've been appropriate, don't you think?"

"That was a bombshell you dropped on me. I told you I needed a minute to process it."

She snatched her hand free. "You had your time."

"I was scared, Talia. I don't want anything to happen to you."

It was all she could do not to snort. Clearly Paul had passed along the whole *Dump Talia* script to Tony, who was now reciting it almost word for word. It was hysterically funny, and she would've laughed if her broken heart hadn't had her in such a stranglehold.

"*You* were scared? Wow. Thanks for explaining that

to me. Because I'm the one with cancer, and I don't know anything about fear. I'm sure *my* fear is nothing compared to *your* fear. Thanks for putting things in perspective for me."

He got up, paced away and came back, running his hands over the top of his head and then dropping them to his sides where his fists flexed with obvious frustration. Opened and closed…opened and closed…until his knuckles whitened and she could see the imprint of his nails in his palms.

"Let me ask you a question." There was a rough edge to him now, as though he was clinging to his civility by the slimmest of spiderwebs. "Why did you stop writing to me?"

A new feeling began to prickle along her spine: dread. "That's a pretty random question, don't you think?"

"No, I don't think. Why did you stop?"

She hesitated, thinking hard for a simple explanation, which refused to materialize. "I—I was with Paul, and I'd just gotten my diagnosis, and I…I—"

"You were scared," he said flatly. "You were starting to feel something for me, and I was a soldier in a war zone and that scared you. You didn't want to get too wrapped up in me if I was going to go off and get myself killed, did you?"

The terrible certainty of truth settled over her, not that she was ready to admit it now or ever. "No," she said too quickly. "That's not true—"

Tony moved up again, positioning himself back in her face. He didn't touch her, but that terrible look in his eyes—part understanding, part recrimination—trapped her just as his hand on her wrist had.

"You weren't worried about what would happen to me? You weren't scared to care too much?"

This time, when she opened her mouth, the denial wasn't so quick to come. "I— Of course not."

"Bullshit."

Another one of those periods of painful silence passed, during which it felt like they were both digging trenches and preparing to settle in for a long and bloody battle. No big deal, right? Battles were fine. God knew she was used to them. What she couldn't deal with was the sudden hot flare of hope burning inside her, as though peace could be an option. As though they might find a way to be together after all.

"What do you want, Tony?"

He shrugged. "That's easy. I want us to get past our mutual bullshit and fear. And I want you."

She shook her head automatically, but the hope had gained a toehold inside her and it didn't feel as though it was going away anytime soon.

"We're a bad fit. We've both got too many issues. I don't see how things can work."

Something in his expression softened, and his eyes crinkled at the edges with the kind of absolute understanding that always made her unravel.

"I'm going to tell you the truth. Even though it makes me look like the world's biggest coward, I'm going to tell you. Okay?"

No. It was not okay. They did not need to head down this path.

"Yeah. Okay."

That hint of a smile faded away, leaving only naked intensity and a man who was having a terrible struggle opening his mouth and getting the words out. She watched, disbelieving, as his nostrils flared and his chin quivered before he pressed his lips together and focused in on all his emotions.

"I've been scared before. Once or twice."

Talia waited, straining to hear him over the heady beat of her heart inside her ears.

"I've never been scared like I was when you told me you had cancer." He swiped a hand under his eyes and nose, whooshing out a harsh breath. "I shut down. It would be easier to go back and spend another year in Afghanistan than to manage my fear of something happening to you, Talia. I'd do anything for you to not have to go through any pain or suffering." He paused, his Adam's apple bobbing. "I don't know how good I can be in a crisis."

Unbidden, Gloria's words came back to Talia.

I'd trade places and be sick for you if I could.

And she stared at Tony, her heart melting.

"I don't plan to die, Tony."

"That's good, because I don't plan to live without you."

Well, that was something, wasn't it? Was it safe to feel hopeful now, or should she make him swear a blood oath?

"I need someone I can count on," she warned him.

"So do I." He let out a shaky laugh. "Because, in case you haven't noticed, I've still got a few post-traumatic stress issues I'm working through."

Staring at him, she felt the wild urge to laugh and cry, all at the same time.

"Oh, well. PTSD. Is that all?"

Another shaky laugh.

"So… Where does this leave us?" she wondered.

"Funny you should ask." Reaching out a hand, he reeled her up and into his arms. "I think it's time for us to get to know each other better and find out."

"Yeah?"

"Yeah." He lowered his head, taking his time moving in for a kiss. "I'm thinking we can get something to eat, and then maybe—"

A sound like a muffled screech startled them, and they looked around in time to see the bedroom door fly open and bang the wall with a thud.

Gloria looked like a trillion bucks in the hot-red dress, except that her face was twisted up with either anger or pain as she marched in and stopped dead when she saw Tony.

"Great." Her voice cracking, she hit him with a glower so dangerous it could probably cause the sun to cool. "It's you."

"Gloria," he murmured. "Always a pleasure."

"What brings you here?" Gloria, who always acted like she owned the place, even if she was standing in the middle of the White House, put her hands on her hips and hiked up her chin until even Talia wanted to take a swing at her. "Have you come to finish breaking my sister's heart?"

"Ah, Gloria." Talia stepped between the two of them before someone threw a punch. "What's wrong? I thought you were leaving for your date."

Gloria choked on something that was either an ugly laugh or a sob. "No, you didn't. You knew he'd stand me up again." Holding up her phone, which evidently had a text on it, Gloria waved it in Talia's face. "Well, now's your chance to rub my face in it. His wife invited friends over for dinner, so he can't get away. What a surprise."

"Ah…" Tony's eyes were now the size of bowling balls. Backing up a step or two and showing every sign of wanting to sprint from the room, he jerked his thumb toward the kitchen. "Why don't I wait in the—"

Gloria turned on him. "Oh, no, you don't. I've got something to say to you."

Oh, hell, no. The last thing she needed was her sister venting all her anger and heartbreak on Tony. True, he'd survived war and torture, but that was nothing compared to Gloria when she let loose with her nasty temper.

"Gloria," Talia spat.

Tony silenced her with a raised hand. "It's okay. I'm anxious to hear whatever Gloria has to say to me."

"I really doubt that," Talia muttered.

They ignored her.

"Go ahead," Tony told Gloria. "I'm listening."

Gloria's lips peeled back in a feral smile. "If you make my sister cry," she said sweetly, "I'm going to cut your balls off with my gardening shears."

Wow. Glo really had a way with people, didn't she?

Tony didn't seem to mind. Unsmiling, he held Gloria's gaze. "Understood."

Gloria, who'd clearly been gunning for a fight, had not gotten her wish, and her face crumpled accordingly. To her credit, though, she recovered quickly and stiffened her spine. "Good."

O-kay, then.

Well, it was great that the two most important people in her life had reached an accord of some sort, but Talia was worried about Gloria. Tears were collecting in her eyes, and she looked so forlorn that Talia really didn't want her to be alone tonight.

Talia opened her mouth, but Tony, bless his heart, beat her to the punch. "Hey, ah, Gloria. If you're not going to, you know, rip my tongue out or anything, why don't you have dinner with us? We're about to—"

This unexpected kindness seemed to take Gloria by surprise. She made another of those choked sounds, and this time there was no question—it was a sob. Gloria stifled it, slapping her hand over her mouth. Talia and Tony exchanged worried looks. After a couple of seconds, Gloria pulled it together enough to drop her hand and flash a smile that was watery but genuine.

"No, thanks," she said. "You two enjoy your date, okay?"

With that, she scurried out of the apartment and down the hallway, but not before they heard the muffled sound of her wail.

"I'll be right back."

Tony watched Talia dash out behind her sister—who was clearly wound pretty tight, wasn't she?—and stood there for a minute, wondering what the hell he should do now. He could help Talia chase Gloria down, of course, but that idea had zero appeal. What would he say if they caught her? Tell her not to worry because the cheating punk would surely leave his wife soon? Yeah…no. Tony did not, as a general rule, engage in emotional displays, and any feelings he had these days should be channeled into keeping his fledgling relationship with Talia on track. Lord knew he had his hands full with that; anything else was above his pay grade.

No. Best to stay here inside the apartment.

As if to second this decision, Chesley ambled over and sat next to him, her tail thumping on the floor. When he was a little too slow on the uptake, the dog nudged his hand with her head, and he scratched her ear. A few seconds of this mutual affection sanded away the rough edges of the tension he'd been feeling. That was the funny thing about dogs, he decided; while you were taking care of them, they took care of you.

So. Talia's apartment.

As always, his curiosity about her got the best of him. He turned in a slow circle, taking inventory. This was a great place. Contrary to what he might've expected based on her choice in hair color, the apartment was quiet and serene. Its pale blue walls, huge windows and ivory sofas and love seats gave the effect of floating in the clouds.

She was fond of art, of course, with paintings lining every inch of the walls. None of them, he realized to his surprise, were hers. In fact…they were all beautifully framed Monet prints of water lilies, which added to the general peace.

She also had a bunch of flower bowls, family photos in fancy frames and stacks of coffee-table books all over the place, including on the marble hearth.

Over on the floor in the corner was a giant pillow with dog toys scattered around it, and the kitchen, on the other side of a granite bar, was full of high-end appliances and copper pots dangling from a ceiling rack.

She cooked, he remembered. She'd mentioned making a fantastic Christmas feast fit for a king in one of her letters to him, hadn't she?

He wanted to be here with her this Christmas Day.

Man, did he want that.

Some of that intensity must have been written on his face, because she did a double take as she hurried back into the apartment, shutting the door behind her.

"What is it?" she asked, arrested.

She was beautiful. Every time he saw her, it surprised him anew.

Today she wore a chin-length wavy black wig that was pretty close to the style she'd had the day he met her. Her sleeveless dress was a blaze of blue that made her skin gleam and did something wonderful with her gray eyes, heightening the color until they sparkled with diamond brilliance. A pretty flush ran over her cheeks, and her plump lips were parted and kissable.

Inside him, need for her swelled and curled, tightened and burned.

She had some kind of crazy effect on him, this one did.

"Tony?"

"Ah." He blinked. "Nothing. How's Gloria? Did you catch her?"

"Yeah, but she insisted on going home. She's a mess right now. As you saw."

"I'm sorry."

She shrugged, looking circumspect. "What can you do? People have to learn their own lessons, don't they?"

"That's very wise." He sat on the arm of the sofa. "Who said that? Aristotle?"

"Talia Adams," she said, grinning.

That smile tied him up in knots every single time. Was that the thing about her that had haunted him all this time? The smile? Or was it the kindness? The wisdom? If he identified what it was, could he root it out? Would he want to, if he could?

Nah. It was too late for any remedial measures like that.

"Really?" He cocked a brow. "And is Talia Adams the genius who told Gloria to get involved with a married man in the first place?"

"Absolutely not. You offend me, sir."

"Is she going to be okay?"

"Okay? If by that you mean that she'll dump the bastard, then no. I don't think she's ready to do that. I want her to, but she won't listen to me. And there's no reasoning with people when they think they're in love, is there?"

That was a question he couldn't answer.

Hell, the way he was feeling right now? It was best to keep his big fat mouth shut.

But he wasn't so good with the poker face. Neither was she.

She stilled, meeting his gaze and reflecting back many of the unruly emotions that churned inside him. "What is it?" she asked again, taking a slow step toward him. "You weren't thinking about Gloria when I came in just now, were you?"

Why lie? "I was thinking about you. It's always you, Talia."

The soft catch of her breath was like a feather across his belly. "I'm not sure I'm worthy of that much thought."

"I'm sure you are."

"Why are you so sure?" she asked quietly.

There was another unanswerable question. He could only shake his head.

"And what were you thinking about me, Tony? When I walked in?"

He opened his mouth, and out came more truth that he'd been prepared to speak.

"I was thinking that I'm trying to rebuild my life and become a solid person. I have nightmares and it doesn't take a whole lot to throw me into a panic attack. Pretty much any sudden loud noise will do it. I'm just starting my career outside the army, and what I know about running an auction house wouldn't fill a thimble. So I'm thinking I may be an abject failure."

"No, you won't—"

"So here's my bottom line. I'm not really a treat for any woman right now. Especially a great woman like you—"

"Tony—"

"—and if I were any kind of man, I'd stay away from you because that's probably best for you, and you deserve nothing but the best."

Some of the light behind her eyes began to dim. "So. This is you saying goodbye?"

"I didn't say that."

A long second passed, during which the air shifted between them and began a slow sizzle that he could almost hear.

She edged closer again, coming within arm's length, and a corner of that delicious mouth curved in the beginnings of a knowing smile. Did she know, then? Did she understand that, as far as he was concerned, she was the reason he'd come home from the war in one piece?

"Then what are you saying?"

He took a deep breath and leaped with his whole heart. "I'm saying I don't want to want you this much."

"But you do."

"Oh, yeah. So I'm going to go with it. If that's okay with you."

She didn't hesitate. "Oh, yeah."

Relief swelled inside him, the sweetest feeling he'd ever known. "Good."

"I have a quote for you. From *Rocky.* You've seen *Rocky,* right? If you haven't, we may have to end things right now."

"I've seen *Rocky.*"

"He's trying to explain his attraction to Adrian, and he says something like, 'Gaps. I got gaps, and she's got gaps, and we fill each other's gaps.'"

"Gaps, eh?"

"Gaps."

Was that the moment? The moment when he knew, without a doubt, that he would marry this woman if she was crazy enough to have him? It sure felt like it.

Staring into those bright eyes of hers, it didn't feel so scary.

"Come here," he told her, opening his arms. "I think we need to discuss *Rocky* a little further."

Chapter 10

Tony's gentle hands caressed her throat. With a serrated sigh, she let her head fall back and her eyes roll closed, happily surrendering her body and anything else he might think to ask for. He ran his thumbs over her veins, searching out her pulse, which had to be in the thousand-beats-per-minute range. When he found it, a low croon of approval vibrated in his chest, and he pulled her closer, until she was standing between his thighs. Gripping his heavy shoulders and hanging on for dear life, she waited…waited…until he leaned in and tipped his face up, pressing his hot tongue to her sensitive flesh.

Need made her cry out.

Happy to indulge her, he planted his hands on her ass and pressed her up against his rigid arousal, taunting her with what she could have if only he'd hurry up.

At the same time, his tongue swirled, teasing her neck with wider and wider circles that made her unravel into more cries…more sensations…more insistent demands.

"Kiss me," she murmured, lowering her head to catch his lips beneath hers. They watched each other, both heavy-lidded and drowsy-eyed, and she caught the groove of his dimples as he smiled, and the pink of his tongue before it slipped into her opening mouth.

Ah, God.

She thrust her own tongue and sucked him deeper, desperate to get him inside her skin and to be inside his. His mouth was slick and minty, and he used every part of it to drive her wild, nipping with his teeth, rubbing with his tender lips and searching with his tongue.

His hips, meanwhile, surged against hers, unerringly hitting that delicious spot between her thighs. His hands held her locked in place, giving her no way to hide from the rising pleasure. She writhed, needing to spread her legs and take all of him inside her, and needing it now.

If he knew it, he didn't care.

"Tony, please," she murmured, digging her nails into his nape.

"Please what?"

"Please don't stop."

"What else?"

"Please touch me."

"Where?"

"Everywhere."

Those eyes gleamed up at her again, laughing now. "Can you be more specific?"

Damn him for making her say it. Why did she have to expose every single part of herself? "Do you want me to draw you a map?"

"I have a pen."

Frustration made her smack him hard on the sculpted slabs of his chest, and he laughed and kissed her again, holding her as she tried to alternately beat him to death and squirm free.

Naturally, he didn't let her go.

Still holding her around the waist, he stood and pressed her back onto the sofa, toppling over on top of her until they were pressed together from head to foot and nothing was funny anymore.

They stared at each other, both panting and startled by the sudden intimacy of the contact. He nipped at her mouth again, but his gaze went to the top of her head. His hands followed.

Oh, God. She knew what was coming.

"Do we need this?" he wondered, tugging at the wig.

Yes, she wanted to say. That wig was a defense that protected her. When she wore it, she didn't have to see a cancer victim in the mirror, nor did she have to endure the pitying stares of strangers when she walked down the street.

Without it, she was… What was she?

Naked? Vulnerable? Mortal?

"You're beautiful," he told her, gently tugging the wig and dropping it to the floor as though it was a meaningless collection of fibers, rather than one of the things that kept her sane and normal. "I don't want hair. I just want you."

To her pained embarrassment, she felt her face crumple, and there she went with the tears during sex. Again. But Tony didn't seem to mind short, curly hair only a quarter inch longer than a buzz cut, and he didn't mind the waterworks, either.

He stared down at her, his face dark and unreadable, and kissed both eyes and both temples. The bridge of her nose. Her forehead. The tip of her chin, and then finally—sweetly—her mouth.

She arched her back, relaxing and melting into the sofa.

Into him.

Into herself.

When he raised his head again, his lips were slick and swollen, and his eyes were also wet. "Where should I touch you?"

Oh, thank God. The rising need had taken her far beyond hesitation or shyness, and she couldn't show him fast enough.

Taking the hand that was still cupping her face, she kissed his fingertips and then lowered it down between them. He shifted a little to one side, and she bent one knee so that the bottom of her skirt rose up to her bare thighs. Moving together, they reached for the waistband of her silky panties, and she lifted her butt so that he could slide them off her legs.

When he'd tossed the panties onto the floor, he skimmed his hands up under her skirt again, brushing his knuckles over the sensitized flesh between her legs until her hips arched. He answered this unspoken invitation by stroking his fingers in her creamy cleft, sending delicious spirals of pleasure to her belly and engorged nipples.

"Tony."

He rubbed her again and again, his touch rhythmic and unerringly running over her aching sex, and she rose and fell against him, involuntarily reaching for her pleasure—

"You know," he said, withdrawing his hand just when one more stroke would have sent her jackknifing into ecstasy, "I think I'll start...*here.*"

Wait, *what?*

Working on her dress from the top down now, he unbuttoned the collar—it was a mandarin style with piping and swirling dragons—and the bodice, slowly exposing her breasts in the sheer black silk of her bra.

And her scar.

Her hands came up automatically, wanting to cover the thick and puckered line where her skin had once been smooth and unmarked, but he caught her hands and lowered them out of his way. That gleaming gaze of his flickered up to her face, flashing a warning.

"Don't."

"But—"

With a smile that was gentle and encouraging, he threw her words right back in her face.

"Gaps, Talia. Remember? I have nightmares. You have scars. We both have gaps. Why can't we help each other?"

Her chin tried to quiver, but she was finished with the tears.

He was right, wasn't he? She'd faced down cancer. She wasn't about to let some freaking little scar prevent her from enjoying the most beautiful experience of her life.

"Oh, you were listening, eh?"

He didn't smile. "I always listen to you. I thought you knew that."

She nodded, not trusting her voice any longer.

"So...is this okay?"

"Anything."

That was all the encouragement he needed. With a low growl of masculine appreciation, he dove in, nuzzling his lips against her scar and loving every inch of it. The intimacy stunned her, trapping the breath in her throat, and there was no chance to recover. A flick of his fingers undid the bra's front clasp, and then he brushed the cups aside, dipped his head and latched on, sucking one aching nipple into the hot center of his mouth.

A shocked, high note shot out of her before she could stifle it, and that drove him on. His mouth on one breast, he massaged the other, squeezing the nipple and then, when she thought she'd pass out if he didn't give her a break, he switched.

Nonsense came out of her in an unstoppable stream.

"Ah, God."

"Tony, you have to—"

"Please. Please. I'm begging you. Don't make me—"

"I can't take it. I can't—"

Finally, he took pity on her. Reaching down between them again, he pressed his fingers to her sex, and she came, going off like a firework with spasming arms, writhing hips and curling toes. Muscles all up and down her body went rigid, arching her backward into the sofa's armrest until it seemed like a possibility that her spine would snap.

Over her subsiding cries and whimpers, she heard Tony's muttered curse and the sound of him fumbling around for something. Spent but determined not to miss anything, she cracked her lids open to see him unzip his pants and sheath his straining erection.

She'd been having trouble catching her breath. Now it got worse in the best possible way. *"Tony."*

Without answering, he gave her a long glance with those gleaming eyes of his. Then he was easing her legs apart and thrusting inside her body, starting the delicious torture all over again.

The only thing she could do was dig her nails into the flexing muscles of his ass and hang on for the relentless ride. He was wild and unabashed, almost frantic with his movements.

Braced on his forearms, he drove harder…deeper… his entire body straining and releasing with each pump of his hips. Tendons pulsed in his neck, and the muscles in his shoulders and chest stood out in stark relief beneath his sweat-slicked skin. Her name poured out of his mouth, hoarse and guttural. And he unerringly hit her swollen and sensitized sweet spot, winding her tighter and sending her higher than she'd ever been before.

Panting and mindless, she glanced down along the length of their moving bodies and saw the contrast between their skin, his dark to her lighter, and the way her legs encased him, holding him inside her body in a death grip, and the way the hard slabs of his chest flattened her breasts.

The intimacy and sensuality of it was overwhelming, and she watched, mesmerized, until—

"Tony."

The pleasure, bright and piercing, shot through her, catching in her throat and lingering there, preventing her from making a sound.

But he knew.

He'd been watching her, and the last thing she saw before he leaned his head back and came with a raw shout, was the hint of smiling satisfaction in his expression.

And then he was rigid in her arms, gasping for air as he murmured her name one last time.

He went still, crushing her into the sofa with his dead weight.

She reveled in it. In him. In the earthiness of this moment, with the sweat and the musk and the pleasure between them.

Now, she decided, was the time.

So she kissed the side of his neck and caressed his nape, easing him back to life.

"Tony?"

"Mmm."

"I went to the doctor today."

His head shot up. He stared at her, the question in his dark eyes, but couldn't seem to speak.

"The scans were all clear."

He swallowed, nostrils flaring, and pressed his lips together.

She smiled, letting the joy fully come for the first time since she'd had her appointment earlier. "The cancer's gone."

"It's...gone?" he echoed, voice cracking.

"Gone."

He blinked.

She waited.

His expression slowly brightened, and a corner of his mouth edged up in a smile in the second before his face crumpled.

And then Tony, her fierce warrior, buried his head in the curve between her neck and shoulder, gathered her closer and sobbed with relief.

* * *

What—?

Talia snapped awake and blinked into her bedroom's darkness, not certain what had woken her. The room was quiet and the clock's digital display indicated dead of night. She rubbed her eyes, wondering if she'd had one of those falling dreams again, and—

Beside her, Tony moaned.

Wait, Tony? Here in her apartment?

She checked the other side of the bed.

Yeah. Tony.

It all came back to her in a rush, and instinct made her spring into action. He'd kicked off the linens and lay on his belly on the farthest edge of the king-size bed, perched at an angle that made her wonder why he wasn't crashing to the floor. His arms and legs twitched. His face twisted. He moaned again, but this time the sound was more urgent, heading into wail territory.

She slid closer to him, flipping the covers back over him as she went. Crooning, she caressed his temple and kissed his cheek and neck, soothing him. His skin was icy, and there was only one solution for that. She stretched out alongside him, protecting him with her arms and legs and keeping him close.

He stilled, his forehead smoothing until he looked so boyish, innocent and vulnerable that it made her heart contract with emotions too overwhelming and frightening to identify.

And then, without warning, his lids flicked open.

He stared at her.

She waited, anxious to see which way this would go.

He smiled.

She gasped out a relieved breath. "You okay?"

"Oh, yeah."

"We're going to work on those nightmares."

A shadow crossed his eyes, but he nodded. Recaptured his smile.

"How does it feel to be back in a bed?" she wondered.

"Your bed? Pretty damn good."

There was a jingle of tags near his side of the bed, and they glanced around to see Chesley. Apparently she'd been sitting patiently, but now, realizing that she had their attention, she whined, asking for permission.

Talia looked to Tony.

"Why not?" he said, scooting over to make room for the dog.

Talia patted the bed and Chesley leaped up, happy to be included. They rearranged themselves, with Tony in the middle, Talia in his arms and Chesley pressed against his back, so that he would be well protected from his demons in the night.

"Here you are," Tony said, late one afternoon three weeks later, tugging his tie a little looser and rolling up the cuffs on his starched dress shirt. It was hotter than a campfire in the Sahara at the pool behind his house in the Hamptons, but well worth it for this particular view of Talia.

Her lips curled into the slow smile that always threatened to drop him to his knees, but she didn't open her eyes. "Was I missing?" she murmured.

"Yeah. I've been in the city for two days. I expected you to be at the front door waiting for me. I'm starting to think you didn't miss me."

Her eyes flicked open, hitting him with the sparkling gray gaze that was so much more fascinating than the waves on the other side of the dunes. "Oh, I missed you."

"I'm not convinced."

"No?"

"No."

Mesmerized by the sight of all that sun-kissed skin, bare except for the black triangle of the string-bikini bottoms that didn't quite manage to cover her perfectly round ass, he sat on the edge of her chaise.

This was, he decided, the perfect ending to his long day full of meetings.

The air was clear and humidity free, the sky the bright blue of aquamarines. A light breeze blew, ruffling the clumps of yellow black-eyed Susans and potted sea grasses that framed the pool area, and a stainless-steel bucket of Corona beers with limes chilled on a side table.

Best of all, his woman was nearly naked and within arm's reach.

Life was, in short, pretty damn good.

Talia, who'd been sunbathing on her belly, levered up on her elbows, causing the untied strings of her bikini top to fall away from the toned curve of her back. She had a beautiful back. He skimmed his fingers down her spine, enjoying the way her skin shivered and her breath caught.

Even better than her back were her breasts, not that they were in sight at the moment. Alas. He had a tantalizing glimpse of them, though, and he stared at where that deep cleavage disappeared against the cushions.

He couldn't see the dark nipples he loved so much.

If only she'd raise herself up a little bit higher—

"How was your support group?" she asked.

As usual, he had mixed feelings about discussing his vets' group with her. The war seemed so far away from what they were building together, and he wanted to keep it that way.

"It was good."

"Yeah?" she said encouragingly.

"But I don't want to talk about it with you."

"Oh."

"Ever."

"Oh."

"Is that okay?"

She gave that some consideration. "As long as I know you're getting the support you need from them."

Yeah, he thought. This one was a keeper.

"Between the group, my shrink and you? I think I'm pretty well covered."

That seemed to satisfy her. "Good."

"But you're in the doghouse," he reminded her. "I don't think you missed me like you should have."

Her face lit with amusement. "What can I do to convince you?"

He shrugged, now running his palm over her plump thighs to her butt, which he massaged with a firm stroke that made pleasure hum in her throat. Tugging gently, he untied the string nearest him.

"I'm not sure you can."

"Oh, no." She pouted, attracting his gaze to her talented and delicious mouth. "But I have some of your favorite beer for you. And it's cold."

"Eh," he said.

Her slow grin stretched wider as she shifted a little

to face him. She rested her head on one hand, and her bracelets clinked. As though she knew how she was winding him up tight, promising heaven but not handing it over, she rested her free arm across her breasts, smooshing them, but still keeping those nipples well out of sight, damn her. On the plus side, the wide curve of her hip was now visible, as was her taut belly.

He could work with that.

"Is that all you have to offer me?" he asked. "The beer?"

"What else do you want?"

He let his gaze sweep over her, all the way down her toned legs to her feet, with the silver toe ring, and then back up to her eyes again. They widened, the black pupils dilating with arousal.

"What do you think I want?" he murmured.

She stared him right in the face. "I'm hoping you want me."

That was about the time his voice got hoarse and he began to sweat. His brain, which had mostly checked out by that point, did manage to hone in on one relevant question.

"Where's Mickey?"

"Oh, didn't I mention? I gave him the night off."

"Good thinking." He paused, savoring the way she could make all his secret nerve endings tingle to life with just a look. "So."

"So." Arching up a little, deepening that sexy curve in her spine and revealing just a bit more of her breasts, she bent her knees so that her feet hovered just above her ass. Her juicy, juicy ass. He swallowed hard, working on his control. "You do want me, right?"

Like a starving man wanted to grab a fork and belly

up to the buffet at Golden Corral. "I don't know," he told her. "Let's see what you've got."

"If you insist."

In a sign of her trust in him and how far they'd come together, she rolled all the way over and eased onto her back, stretching her arms high overhead. He watched as her full breasts bounced and settled into those perfect, chocolate-tipped ovals. The scar, like everything else about her, was beautiful, because it meant that the monster had been cut out of her body, leaving her here to live her life.

With him.

He stilled, his heaving lungs generating a slow sigh.

Her clear-eyed gaze saw it all, and her smile faded as she reached for him. "You're not going to just stand there, are you?"

He managed a head shake. "No."

His plan was to stretch out atop her, but she had other ideas. He knelt on the chaise and she rose up to meet him, her lips already parting and giving him a glimpse of her moist tongue. With the kind of low growl that probably belonged behind bars at the zoo, he dragged her up against him, filling his hands with as much of her sweet flesh as he could hold.

Their kiss was deep and urgent, and he unraveled completely.

"You have no idea what you do to me," he told her between sucks and nips. "I need you."

"I need you, too."

That wasn't enough. He grabbed her upper arms, slowing her down so she'd look into his face and see how serious he was. Her eyes, half-closed and sultry, met his gaze and her swollen lips parted in surprise.

Yeah, he was feeling pretty intense right about now.

"Don't you ever leave me," he continued. "I can't live without you. You know that, don't you?"

She hesitated.

He squeezed her arms. "Don't you?"

"Yes. *Yes.*"

Thank God. Relief made it easier for him to suck in a couple of desperately needed breaths, but then she went to work on him.

Pushing him down on his back, she unbuckled his belt and undid his pants, no easy feat given the size of his erection at this point. Her face was dark with concentration as she rearranged his boxer briefs, easing him free and fisting him in her tight grip.

"Talia," he said, choked.

She lowered her head, taking him inside her mouth's slick heat. He tried to say her name again, but all that came out was a half-strangled moan. She wrung him out—bobbing and sucking, making a vibrating croon in her throat that heightened all of his sensations—until he was so far gone he wouldn't have noticed if a bagpiper in full regalia had marched out playing "Danny Boy."

At the last possible second, sanity intruded.

He'd been gripping her head—gently, he hoped—and now he tugged a little and she looked up at him, a brow raised in question.

"Inside you," he croaked. "I need to be inside you."

With that woman's gleam of satisfaction bright in her eyes—yeah, he was good and whipped, and she had to know it—she rose up, straddling him.

And fumbling as though he wore leather gardening

gloves, he grabbed her ass to anchor her and eased her down onto him.

They both gasped, taking a moment to settle together. Bracing herself on her elbows so that her breasts rested against his chest, she stared down at him. He, meanwhile, stared up at her, keeping a tight grip on her hips as they began to swivel.

Before he went completely deaf, dumb and brainless, he decided that they needed to make a plan or two.

"I saw the mural when I got home."

"The mural?" she gasped, her head tipping back.

"It's finished. It's fantastic."

"Hmm," she said, sitting up and cupping her breasts as though offering them to him.

Man. He loved it when she did that.

Okay. Time to talk faster.

"So we'll be moving to the city next week, right? So you can work on the mural at Davies & Sons."

With what looked like great difficulty, she cracked her eyes open and frowned down at him. "Why are you talking?" she demanded.

"I'm thinking that since Arianna and her family are staying at the penthouse for now, you and I can live at your apartment." He paused, giving the words time to sink in. "If that works for you."

She blinked, and then a glorious smile spread across her face as she went back to what she'd been doing, riding him hard.

"Yeah," she said. "That works for me."

Chapter 11

It was the biggest night of her professional life, Talia thought three months later, as she wove, champagne flute in hand, through the glittering, black-tie crowd. She couldn't dislodge the hard knot of fear in her throat.

For one thing, she could hardly believe that she was here in such an opulent setting, and no one was kicking her out. Candles flickered on giant candelabras. Giant arrangements of flowers—Casablanca lilies, gardenias, hydrangeas and other exotic blooms that looked as if they cost five dollars or more per stem—graced round bowls on every horizontal surface. Uniformed servers marched back and forth with trays filled with caviar points and lobster thingies that she didn't know the names for, but she was too frazzled to eat. The general hubbub was intensified by the sounds of a jazz combo playing somewhere nearby, and she could feel the beginnings of a tension headache tightening the back of her neck. A single thought kept running through her mind: these might be Tony's people, but they sure weren't hers.

Still, they all went out of their way to make her feel welcome, and that was another thing that had her so rattled.

The kudos came from every direction, so many they made her head spin.

Someone touched her arm. Turning, she saw a well-known Manhattan socialite, a woman active on the board of the Museum of Modern Art and so wealthy that she could fly to Paris to order her spring wardrobe from the couture shows or write a six-figure check for a painting without breaking stride.

The woman's beaming smile was barely visible over the blinding glare from her diamond choker. "The mural is stunning, darling. Brilliant job. I'd love to have you around for lunch one day next week. I have a wall in my apartment I'd like you to do something about. I'm going to look at my calendar and give you a call."

Talia worked hard on being nonchalant and getting her bulging eyes back in her head. Was this what happened when the Davies family gave you their seal of approval? Millionaires suddenly knew your name, christened you with endearments and wanted to hire you?

"That'd be wonderful," Talia managed to say. "I'm looking forward to it."

The woman swooped in for an air kiss that breezed by Talia's cheek, then continued on her way.

Talia tried to catch her breath.

Maybe if she ducked into the ladies' room for a minute—

A prickle of awareness tingled down her bare arms, and she looked across the atrium, to Tony. Catching her eye, he winked. Smiled.

He stood with his family in front of the mural, and she knew he wanted her to meet the newcomers, including his sister, Arianna, and his fraternal twin, Sandro. And she would, in a minute.

For now, she needed a minute.

It would help if Gloria were here. The party was now in full swing and there was no sign of her, which didn't bode well, as the two of them had never missed an important night in each other's lives.

Maybe she should text her again, Talia thought, digging in her beaded bag for her cell phone as she skirted the crowd and edged into the ladies' room. As expected, it was a decadent minispa for women, with expensive lotions and other personal items laid out on the counter for the guests' use. It was also empty, which gave Talia the chance to—

Oh, shit.

A woman was crying quietly in the single stall. Her sister, Gloria, to be exact. There was no mistaking the familiar sobbing *ah-ah-ah* noise she made, and Talia ought to know because she'd heard the sound often enough since Gloria had taken up with that married bastard.

Talia sent up a quick prayer for empathy and patience, but none seemed forthcoming. This was just freaking great. As if she needed this drama on top of everything else.

"Gloria." She tapped on the stall and tried to keep

her voice in the soothing range. "It's me. What happened, girl?"

The lock slid free and the door banged open, revealing a woman just this side of distraught. She also smelled yeasty, which would probably explain the empty champagne flute on the counter by the hair spray.

Oh, man. This was bad.

Talia put a hand on her arm and squeezed in what she hoped was a supportive manner. "Glo?"

Jerking free, Gloria stalked over to the console beneath the mirror to snatch a tissue from the box, no easy feat with her questionable blood alcohol level and four-inch heels. It would take more than a few little dabs to get rid of all that tarry black mascara, but she'd probably started out looking drop-dead gorgeous. She was in black, of course, a sleeveless and backless number that accented her legs and ass, and Gloria had plenty of both. But her eyes were bloodshot and her nose red and swollen. To top it all off, she couldn't seem to catch her breath or control her shaking shoulders.

"H-here." She thrust her cell phone at Talia.

Talia glanced at the display, braced for the worst.

I don't want to hurt you, read the message from Aaron Madden. *But I want to be straight with you. Now that Jerri and I are going ahead with the divorce, I feel like I need some time to get myself together. I'm not ready to commit to anything. I think we should see other people.*

A fuzzy red haze of anger made the words run together a little at the end, so Talia read the message again. That was no better. By the third pass, she'd recovered enough to pick her jaw up off the floor and ask an outraged question.

"Are you telling me," she said, between gritted teeth, "that son of a bitch finally left his wife, but he wants the freedom to screw other women? Is that the bottom line here?"

By now, Gloria had clamped down on most of her emotions, but her eyes still had a dangerous glint in them. For the first time ever, Talia wondered what her sister was capable of at a time like this and whether it might include hurting herself or someone else—or someone's property, like, say, a sleek Mercedes sedan.

"That's the bottom line," Gloria said.

"What are you going to do?" Talia asked.

She was temped to launch into a lecture, starting with *I told you so* and ending with *So you're never going to see him again, right?* but they'd been down that road before, several times, and it never ended well for Talia. Inevitably, Gloria reconciled with Aaron and told Aaron that Talia had badmouthed him, which led to a prolonged period of estrangement between the sisters.

After being burned by this process, Talia had learned her lesson. Gloria had to come to her own conclusions about her dysfunctional romantic relationship. Even if they were wrong.

"Do?" Gloria reached for her empty champagne flute and headed for the door. "Well, for starters, I'm going to drink some more champagne. A magnum should do it, don't you think?" Bitterness made her face hard and thinned her mouth into a sneer. "And then I'm going to see if there's anyone interesting in the crowd tonight."

They'd walked out of the bathroom and back into the

crowded chaos of the party, but at this piece of news, Talia stopped dead and wheeled around, causing Gloria to plow into her.

"Anyone interesting?" Talia echoed. "What the hell does that mean?"

Shrugging, Gloria pulled some lip gloss out of her clutch and applied a fresh coat. "Aaron wants me to see other people, right? I'm going to see other people. No time like the present."

This announcement really threw Talia for a loop. Every time she thought she'd seen the outer limits of Gloria's self-destructive behavior, Gloria whipped something new out of her hat to surprise her.

"Oh, no, you're not." Getting jostled by a passing guest, Talia grabbed Gloria's arm and pulled her behind a potted palm, out of the line of traffic. "I'm not going to stand by while you do something you'll regret tomorrow."

"Regret?" Gloria's brows rose. "What? You mean like wasting years of my life on a married man? That kind of regret?"

"Yeah. I'm going to put you in a taxi."

"I don't want to get in a taxi." Gloria snatched another glass of champagne off the tray of a server. "I want to have some fun."

Talia took the glass, dumped the contents into the palm tree, and handed the flute back to Gloria. "You've had enough fun. I'd take you home myself, but I can't just leave—"

"Ladies," said a new voice. "Is something wrong?"

Startled, they turned to see Cooper Davies standing there, having apparently materialized out of nowhere. Unlike the other men present, he wore a dark suit and dark shirt combo rather than a tux, not that it mattered. He looked effortlessly sophisticated, as though he'd rolled out of bed after a late-afternoon romp, swiped just enough gel through his blond curls to tame the thatch across his forehead, thrown on his clothes and come to the party. He was, Talia had already decided, sparing with his smiles, and right now was no exception. His full lips looked grim, his nose hawkish and his blue eyes stormy.

He was looking at Gloria, not Talia, and his intent gaze gave her a thorough once-over.

Since Gloria had progressed to opening a compact and powdering her nose, Talia decided to answer for her. "Gloria has, ah, decided to leave the party—"

"No, I haven't," Gloria interjected loudly.

"—and I'm going to throw her into a cab and send her home, so we're all good. Thanks."

Cooper considered this, brows lowering. "I don't think she should go anywhere by herself."

Yeah, Talia had already considered that issue. With her luck, the second the cab pulled away from the curb, Gloria would direct him to some club or other, where God knew what could happen next. In the mood Gloria was in right now? Hell. Talia wouldn't put it past her to hook up with some idiot in a nightclub and elope to Vegas on the next available flight.

"I know," Talia agreed, "but I can't leave the party yet, and I'm not sure—"

"I can see her home," Cooper said.

"—that I can— Wait, what?"

"I can see her home," Cooper repeated, his gaze finally flickering to Talia's face.

Talia hesitated. This guy was a Davies, which meant

he probably wasn't a rapist or ax murderer, but, on the other hand, they barely knew him and Gloria was clearly not in her right mind.

"Well…"

A hint of amusement made Cooper's eyes crinkle at the edges. "She's safe with me. Don't worry."

"I'm not sure you're safe with her, frankly," Talia muttered.

Cooper laughed, a startling event that flashed his dimples and white teeth.

Gloria, who hadn't been listening, closed her compact with a snap. "What's the plan? Who's coming to the bar with me?"

"You're not going to the bar," Talia said flatly. "Cooper is taking you home."

"Taking me home?" Gloria looked him up and down with significantly more interest, her eyes narrowed and speculative.

"Making sure you get home," Cooper clarified, taking her elbow. "Ready?"

"Hang on. Thanks, Cooper. You're a lifesaver." Rising on her tiptoes, Talia whispered in his ear under the guise of kissing his cheek. "And if you take advantage of my sister while she's drunk, I'm going to clip your balls, fry them up in a beer batter and serve them to you with hot sauce. *Comprende?*"

Another disarming laugh, followed by something that sounded suspiciously like a pledge. "Oh, I *comprende.* And since my balls are very important to me, you won't have to worry about me taking advantage of Gloria. Ever."

Strangely reassured, Talia nodded and moved aside so they could go.

Whereupon Gloria surprised her with a new show of emotion and a piece of sisterly advice as she swiped at her eyes again. "Learn from my mistakes, okay, Tally? Don't bother counting on a man. They never come through in the end."

These two, Tony thought, were really crazy. In a good way.

Arianna and Joshua, who apparently had zero faith in the sitter they'd hired for the night, had spent most of the evening on the phone with her, tracking Apollonia's progress and calling with additional instructions every few minutes.

Tony sighed, watching his sister with bemusement.

She wore a pretty blue dress that matched Joshua's bow tie and cummerbund, and had her hair all done up. Listening intently, with the cell phone pressed to her ear, she shot Joshua a worried look.

Joshua froze, his tumbler of Scotch on the rocks halfway to his lips. *"What?"*

Arianna's eyes were wide, her expression dire. "She says the baby hasn't burped yet."

Joshua frowned. "Well, did she put her over her shoulder or across her lap? Because the lap thing always works for me. Let me talk to her."

Arianna put her index finger up, holding him off as she spoke into the phone again. "Did you put her across your lap?" She nodded, listening. "Well, because that always—"

"And did you ask about the poop?" Joshua interjected. "Did she poop yet? Let me talk to her."

Oh, for God's sake, Tony thought, rolling his eyes and trying not to laugh in their faces, which would probably be rude. These two were going to tackle each other for the phone in a minute.

There she was. About damn time.

"Hi," Talia said, materializing out of nowhere. "What'd I miss?"

Reaching out an arm, Tony gripped the wide curve of her hip, scooped her away from the jostling crowd and nestled her up against his side. He'd developed the habit of always wanting her around so they could confer about breaking events at any given time. It was as though nothing ever really got started, or could be fully enjoyed, until Talia was there with him.

He kissed her temple. "Only these two driving the babysitter crazy."

Arianna, still listening to the phone, spied Talia, smiled and waved like a maniac.

Talia grinned back. "It's the new-parent thing, I suppose."

"Yeah, well, wait'll you see Apollonia," he told her. "She's beautiful. She's got this little Mohawk thing going on with her hair. And she's laughing now. If you give her a raspberry on her cheek—she's got these huge chipmunk cheeks—she'll go crazy."

Wow. Was that him, gushing about a baby like that?

"Oh, she sounds adorable."

Tony kissed her temple again, enjoying the feel of her. In what he considered a major coup, he'd convinced her not to wear a wig tonight and embrace her natural hair, which was growing into lush curls that he loved to finger. She'd worn this sexy-ass dress that was stretchy and purple, with long sleeves and a high neck in front. But in back—whoa. In some amazing feat of modern engineering, there was pretty much nothing, which meant that her toned back was bare all the way down to the twin dimples above her butt.

He couldn't wait to get her home, to say the very least.

And the engagement ring in his breast pocket—a blazing emerald, because a woman like Talia, who was all about color, needed something more interesting than a diamond—was weighing pretty heavy right now. Tonight was the night. Perfect, right? She was the woman of the hour, with all of New York here to appreciate the brilliance of her mural, and such a special night required a very special ending.

Yeah, he couldn't wait.

"How do you feel about children?" he murmured in her ear.

She stiffened a little, her smile fading even as she gave the answer he'd hoped to hear. "I love them."

There it was again. The uneasy vibe he'd been getting from her all evening hit him again, and that shadow streaked across her eyes. Something was definitely up, and it worried him. He'd have to get to the bottom—

"Sorry about that," Arianna announced, hanging up at last and extending a hand to Talia. "I'm Arianna. I'm so thrilled to meet you. Tony's told me all about—"

Uh-oh. No telling where that could go.

"Yeah, okay, moving on," Tony interjected. "This is Arianna's husband, Joshua."

Joshua shook Talia's hand, his eyes bright with subtle masculine appreciation behind his glasses. "How're you doing?"

"It's great to meet you both," Talia told them. "I hear Apollonia's a real looker."

"She's perfect," Arianna gushed with a new mother's pride. "Well, not perfect, actually, because she hasn't burped or pooped yet. So we're, you know, going to have to leave."

Tony's bottom jaw hit the polished floor. What the hell had happened to his sister, who imparted this information with so much gravity you'd think the kid had been diagnosed with a raging case of tuberculosis? "*Leave?* Are you kidding me? The party's just getting started. I think the babysitter can handle—"

"Well, apparently she can't, man." Joshua tossed back the rest of his drink and clinked the empty glass on the tray of a passing server. "Because if she could, Apollonia would have taken care of her business by now. It was nice meeting you, though," he told Talia. "Enjoy the party. The mural's, ah, colorful."

That made Talia grin. "It's called *Sol Resurrection,* by the way. The sun is being reborn."

They all turned to stare at the mural, which was glorious. The best work of Talia's Tony had ever seen, no question, and the perfect antidote to the heartbreaking paintings of her dark period. It was as though she'd taken all the exuberance and light of her personality and distilled it into her slashes and swirls, creating something breathtaking. Tony loved it. But of course, he loved her.

"Well, I saw the sun. I got that much." Color crept up Joshua's cheeks. "Art's not really my thing. But if you want to buy commercial real estate, you let me know."

Talia laughed. "That's a deal. Have a good night. And I hope that, ah, Apollonia's poop comes out okay." She scrunched up her face. "Wow. I don't think I've ever said that to anyone before."

As Arianna and Joshua left, Tony checked his watch. "I really thought Sandro would be here by now. I guess I should check my phone. He might've left me a text— Speak of the devil. There they are."

Mickey appeared through the crowd first, or maybe it was just that he was so hard to miss. Upon seeing them, his face split in a grin that threatened to swallow his entire head. He wore an unfortunate shiny gray tuxedo of the type last seen when the Temptations appeared on *The Ed Sullivan Show,* and yet it was somehow perfect for him. The fire engine-red tie was a startling accessory.

Tony made a face and rubbed his eyes. "You need to give me a warning, man."

Mickey's grin never faltered. "Don't hate. You look fantastic, Talia. What're you doing with this punk when there's a man like me in the world?"

"I ask myself that every day," Talia replied solemnly. "Is that Sandro behind you?"

"This is Sandro." Tony pulled his twin in for a hug, and they slapped each other on the back. "What the hell, man? You folks were supposed to be here an hour ago."

Sandro, who wore a standard black tuxedo, thank goodness, shrugged. "Bad weather out of D.C. And I left you a message, which you'd know if you ever checked your phone. Is this the famous Talia?"

"This is Talia," Tony said, feeling an unwelcome twinge of…unease.

Which was ridiculous, he knew. True, his former fiancée, Skylar, had taken one look at Sandro and fallen out of love with Tony, but that was a whole different situation. He and Sky had been caught up in a whirlwind romance that had been intensified by his pending deployment, and they'd never known each other as they should. And his feelings for Talia now versus what he thought he'd had with Sky?

No comparison. Not even close.

So it was ridiculous to feel uneasy just because Talia and Sandro were now shaking hands and smiling at each other.

Completely ridiculous.

But the thing was—

Skylar's falling in love with Sandro had been a nasty pinch to his ego.

If *Talia* left him, on the other hand...

Whoa. Ugly filled him up inside. He didn't even want to go there.

Talia seemed to know something of what he was feeling. She kept her free hand around Tony's waist and gave him a squeeze as she teased Sandro.

"The less attractive and talented Davies twin. So nice to meet you at last. I don't know why we never met when you dropped Nikolas off for his art lessons."

"Weird, huh?" Sandro laughed, taking the ribbing with good grace. "I like this one, man."

"Don't like her too much," Tony muttered.

Still laughing, Sandro slung an arm around his teenage son, Nikolas, and pulled him into the conversation. "You remember Nikolas, right, Talia?"

"Of course." Talia accepted Nikolas's kiss on the cheek. Nikolas, who was wiry and seemed to have grown a foot every time Tony saw him, had switched his hair from red to blue. No wonder he and Talia got along so well, Tony thought. "How's the painting coming, Nikolas? You're still painting, right?"

Nikolas shrank into the typical teenager slouch, shoving his hands deep into his pockets. "Pretty good. I've been doing some work with charcoals."

"And photography," Sandro added. "He's been doing some great work in black-and-white. Taking pictures of all the national monuments. Tell them, Nik."

Nikolas almost smiled at this praise from his father, but then he caught himself and reverted to an indifferent shrug. "I've got a new Nikon. It's pretty cool. You know."

"I'd love to see your pictures." Talia beamed at him. "I'm so proud."

"Get a grip," Nikolas told her, still working on stifling his grin.

Talia punched his arm. "Where's Skylar?" she asked.

Sandro looked around. "She was going to the ladies'— Oh, there she is."

Skylar floated out of the crowd, smiling and gorgeous in a pale pink gown that—

Whoa. Tony did a double take, even as she saw him.

"Tony," she cried.

"Hello, beautiful." Conscious of the situation's awkwardness and how Talia must be feeling to meet his former fiancée, he rested his hand low on Talia's bare back as he leaned in to kiss Sky on the cheek. "This is Talia."

"Talia," Sky repeated. The women exchanged reserved smiles, and then Sky, God bless her, pulled Talia in for a hug and kiss. "It's so great to meet you."

"I know," Talia said when they separated, laughing now. "I've been wanting to tell you—thank you for dumping Tony."

"My pleasure," Sky said, winking at Tony. "You take good care of him, okay?"

"Absolutely."

"Ah, Sky," Tony began, eyeing the half basketball she seemed to be sporting under her dress, "is there anything, ah, new?"

"Nooo." Sky made a show of furrowing her brow and looked to Sandro. "Is there anything new, Sandro?"

Sandro did the same thing, scrunching his face up with mock puzzlement. "No, I don't think— Well, there is that one thing…"

"Will you two knock it off?" Nikolas leaned across them, cutting his father off and adding an eye roll for effect, even though he was grinning. "Sky's pregnant," he announced. "It's a boy."

"What?"

"That's wonderful!"

This news generated a new round of hugs and back slaps, with much excited chatter about nausea, due dates and nurseries. When the smoke finally cleared, Sandro took his clan off to the buffet table for some chow, and Tony kept Talia in his arms because this was a wonderful night and he couldn't wait another second.

"Wow," she breathed. "What a night—"

"I'm in love with you," he told her. "Marry me."

Talia froze, her smile dying right before his eyes, which was not the thing a man wanted to happen when he put it all on the line like that. Even worse, some darkness reached out and took her from him, extinguishing the light in her personality.

"I—I don't know what to say."

Sudden fear made his voice sharp. "That's easy. Say yes."

"We need to talk about this later, Tony—"

Later was probably a good idea. They were in the middle of a huge freaking party, after all, not the place where you wanted to have what was turning out to be a heart-wrenching conversation. People surrounded them on all sides, the music was too loud and there was no privacy to be had.

But he couldn't wait, so he asked the question that had been niggling at him all night. "What's going on? What's happened?"

She tried that delaying tactic again. "Let's get through the party, and then we—"

"Now."

Her haunted eyes seemed to take up her entire face as she kicked his world out from under him.

"I found a lump this morning. I think the cancer's back."

Chapter 12

They got through the rest of the gala somehow.

A million lifetimes later, what had turned into a nightmare evening was finally over and they climbed into a limo and headed back to Talia's apartment. He stared out his window at the city's glittering lights; she stared out hers. The car stopped. She murmured something. They got out. There were stairs, so he climbed them. A door opened, so he walked through it. The dog licked his hand, so he petted her.

None of it really existed.

For him, only the waking terror was real. It blinded him. Trapped him. Stopped his breath.

What, then, must it be doing to Talia?

They stared at each other, both locked behind something that felt insurmountable. He wanted to reach for her, but his hands had long ago turned to blocks of ice frozen to the ends of his arms. He wanted to speak, but what words could sooth or address...*this?*

They stared at each other across the length of her living room.

"Tell me—" He paused to clear the frog from his throat. "Start from the beginning."

Jesus. He almost couldn't look at her, seeing his own fear mirrored back in those beloved gray eyes.

"There's a lump in my neck. I felt it this morning in the shower."

"And you're just telling me—?"

"I didn't want to ruin the gala," she said simply.

"And I didn't want you to carry this by yourself." Man. That edge in his voice was getting sharper by the moment, wasn't it? "I thought we'd established that, Talia. I thought we were partners in this. You think I'm okay with having the time of my life while you're scared shitless? Does that seem fair to you?"

It took her way too long to answer. "I didn't want to see that look on your face."

Well, he knew that feeling, didn't he?

"Where is it? Show me."

"Why do we need to—"

"Show me."

Moving in super slow motion, she raised a hand to her neck, felt and pointed. "Here."

Jesus. His hands were shaking. Reaching out, he pressed his hand to her warm skin and—

There it was, knotted and hard. Foreign. New.

Was this the thing that would kill her and rob him of the greatest happiness he'd ever known, then? Their own personal Taliban that they couldn't see to fight?

He snatched his hand away, trying not to see the misery in her expression.

"So." His voice was getting more hoarse by the syllable. "Doctor."

"Monday at eight-thirty."

He nodded. That was the best they could do, he supposed. They couldn't very well storm her oncologist's home, demanding a Saturday-night appointment, could they?

"I'll be with you."

She said nothing, which wasn't good for his morale.

A terrible moment passed, full of silence, distance and stark terror.

"Well," she finally said, edging toward the bedroom. "It's late. I'm going to bed. Are you staying?"

Speaking of not good for his morale...

"Excuse me? Did you just ask if I was staying? Is this a joke?"

"You don't have to."

What the hell was going on here? "Try this on for size, Talia—I want to."

Her brows flattened and she made a little *tsk*ing sound. "Do you?"

"What?"

"It's not like we're in the mood for making love, is it? You can barely look at me, and just now you acted like you'd dipped your hand in nuclear waste, so I don't think you'll be touching me at all. Why don't you spend the night in your penthouse—"

"Don't do this, Talia."

She pulled a blank face that made him want to smash something. "Do what?"

"Push me away. I told you I loved you tonight. Did you hear that? I asked you to marry me—"

"Yeah, but that was before you knew—"

He held up a finger to stop her, too choked to speak and too angry to risk hearing another nonsensical word that might come out of her mouth. "Before…I knew? What? That you were human? That you might get sick one day?"

"Might get sick?" she cried. "Are you serious right now? *Skylar* might get sick—"

"Skylar?"

"*You* might get sick. *Sandro* might get sick. Me? I probably *will* get sick. You should find another woman and hedge your bets against the whole *sick* thing."

"I don't want another woman. I thought you knew that. One of your letters talked about 'the one' being the person who was the sun in your life. Well, in case you hadn't noticed, you're that for me. And I will be with you through this—"

That seemed to be too much for her. "Through this?" she shrieked, tendons straining in her neck as she made a sound that was way too ugly to be a laugh. "How noble! What do you think this is, *Love Story?* What're you—Ryan O'Neal? You think I'm going to get sick off camera and then graciously climb into bed and die—"

"Don't say that!"

"—while my cheeks are still dewy and my hair is long and thick? Please!"

"Talia—"

"Have you ever seen someone vomit after chemotherapy, Tony? Ever seen the mouth sores or the radiation burns? Ever seen hair fall out in clumps?" Here she paused for another of those nasty laughs. "Although, to be fair, I don't really have enough hair for it to fall out in clumps, but still—"

"What do you want me to say? No, I've never seen any of that, but I will. If that's what we have to go through to build our life together, then, yeah—"

"Well, let's talk about that for a minute." She marched up to get in his face, her features wild and contorted. "Let's say I do get through another round of treatment and we do get married."

"Hallelujah."

"What if the treatments make me infertile? What if I already am infertile? Did you ever think of that? How're you going to get the babies you seem to want with a wife who can't produce them?"

She didn't really think that was a dilemma, did she?

The ridiculousness of the question made him snort. "If it's a choice between life with you, however it goes, or life with some brood mare, then I'll take you. What else have you got to throw at me?"

She checked herself in surprise. "What's that supposed to mean?"

"It means you can't seem to get rid of me fast enough. You were so worried about me walking out, but you don't get a free pass. I don't walk out on you, and you don't walk out on me. Period. That's the deal. So you'd better dial back that fear."

Her brows snapped together with outrage or bravado—he couldn't tell which—and she puffed up, reminding him of some creature on Animal Planet executing its most effective defensive maneuver.

"Don't you dare."

Calm washed over him, as though God had touched a finger to his head, and he knew, absolutely and irrevocably, that nothing would prevent him from being with this woman until the day one of them died.

He'd been afraid before, and he was afraid now.

But he would work through his fear. He had to.

"You're the coward here, not me," he said quietly. "You're the hypocrite here, not me."

These truths were too much for her. Tears that had been welling for the last several minutes began to fall, wetting her cheeks as she began to sob.

"I want you to leave! Get out of here! Leave me alone!"

Shaking his head, he stretched out on the couch, covered himself with the throw and stared her in the face. "I love you. I'm not going anywhere. Ever."

"We're a little early, I think," Gloria said on Monday morning, keeping her firm grip on Talia's elbow as she steered them off the elevator at the medical arts building and down the long hallway to the oncologist's office. "I told you we had time to stop for coffee."

Though she was so numb that just walking was like trying to run a marathon while under the effects of a sleeping pill, Talia tried to smile. Tried to engage. "You don't need any more coffee. Your bladder's going to explode."

"Eh. You may be right."

Take a step, Talia. Another step. And another.

"We'll get through this, Tally."

"I know. I'm glad you're here. Thanks for—"

Gloria stopped cold. "If you thank me for coming with you, Talia Adams, I swear to God I'll kill you myself."

Uh-oh. Nothing like a death threat to make you change course.

"—finally telling me what happened with you and Cooper Davies when he took you home after the party. And don't deny it. I know you. You've been acting funny."

Predictably, Gloria clammed up, making a show of turning away and staring out the windows as they continued walking. "I don't know what you're talking about," she said flatly.

"I'll get it out of you eventually."

A man stepped around the corner, blocking them.

Oh, God. It was Tony.

She hadn't seen him since Saturday night. In one of her lowest moments, ever, she had walked out on him. Just grabbed her purse, leashed the dog and taken them both with her as she fled to Gloria's apartment, where she stayed, ignoring his frequent calls and texts the entire weekend.

Now here he was. He looked terrible, with ringed eyes, a stubbled chin and wrinkled clothes. If she had any question about whether their brief separation had been as hard on him as it had been on her, here was the proof, in his haunted expression.

Her hand flew to her heart, which had stopped.

His hands, which were down by his sides, rose a little, in a supplicating gesture, as though his words weren't working any better than hers were at the moment.

Please.

Shame hit her hard, because of course everything he'd said to her was right. About her hypocrisy? About her cowardice? True. All, sadly, true.

She'd been so afraid he'd reject her that she hadn't given him a chance, and she was ashamed of herself.

"I'm sorry," she whispered. "I'm so sorry."

His breath hitched. "You should be. Come here."

They came together, hard, and Talia held on to Tony, her anchor, for all she was worth. How on earth had she thought she could make it through this without his quiet strength backing her up?

Gloria slipped away, although Talia could hear her discreet sniffles.

She pulled back so she could see Tony's face. "I love you. I should have told you before."

He nodded, ducking his head as he swiped his eyes. "Yeah. You should've."

"I'm scared," she admitted.

"So am I."

Some of the weight in her chest lifted. Thank God he gave her naked honesty and not some rah-rah speech about how they'd kick cancer's ass. She couldn't take that right now. He was right, of course. Some burdens needed to be shared.

"I have a quote," she told him. "From Dr. King."

Those dimples appeared in his cheeks. "Oh, yeah? I could use a quote right about now. Hit me."

"He said, 'We must build dikes of courage to hold back the flood of fear.'"

Tony nodded. "'Dikes of courage.' That works for me. I've got a big shovel and a strong back."

"God, I love you."

"I love you, too, baby," he said, kissing her temple a last time.

"Well." She worked up a smile that felt reasonably courageous. "Should we go? I don't want to be late."

"Not just yet."

He reached inside his jeans pocket and produced something small.

Then he reached for her left hand.

Covering her mouth with her free right hand, trying not to erupt in tears, Talia watched as he slipped a ring on her finger. It was the brightest green emerald imaginable, surrounded by diamond baguettes.

When it was safely on her finger, Tony took her hand and, followed by Gloria, who was sniffling louder than ever now, led her into the doctor's office.

"Now we're ready."

Epilogue

Twenty years later

As though he knew that repressed tears were about to make her nostrils flare and her chin tremble, Tony took her hand, lacing her fingers in his strong grip.

She squeezed back, grateful for the support.

They walked on, across the blazing green lawn of The Plain.

It was R-Day. Reception Day. Already. Where had the time gone?

The weather couldn't have been more perfect, with its light breeze, clear blue sky and bright—but thankfully not hot—sunlight. The setting? Indescribably beautiful. The Hudson River, a sparkling gray today, stretched before them and those craggy hills surrounded it on either side. They'd visited some gorgeous colleges in the last year or so, yeah, but this one, as far as she was concerned, took the cake.

She sighed, feeling that sweet ache around her heart again.

Without breaking stride, Tony raised her hand to his lips and pressed it with a lingering kiss.

Talia gave him a sidelong glance. This, naturally, made him grin with happiness that was both crazy and peaceful.

He had gray at his temples now, and interesting lines fanning out from the corners of his eyes and bracketing his mouth when he smiled. He was, in other words, handsomer and more intriguing than he'd been the day they met, and she loved him more every day. If someone had told her that this would be possible back when they'd gotten married, she'd have convulsed with laughter, but it was true.

"Congratulations, baby," he told her, smoothing a strand of her windswept curls, which had grown back longer and more luxuriant than ever, out of her face.

"For what?" she asked, even though she knew. "Not killing the boy when he let his pet tarantula loose in the living room so it could stretch its legs?"

"No," Tony said, unsmiling. "For hitting your twentieth anniversary today."

The day's poignancy snuck up on her again, choking her up a little, but she nodded. Twenty healthy, cancer-free years. With Tony. "God is good, isn't he?"

Tony swiped at his eyes with his free hand. "God is good."

Their joy bubbled over in mutual laughter, and they let it come.

Then she checked her watch and decided they'd better pick up their step.

"If you're finished being mushy on me, we'd better get going. We don't want to be late for the ceremony, do we?"

"Hell to the no," he agreed. "Alexios would kick both our butts."

Still laughing, their arms swinging between them, they headed for their seats to watch their eighteen-year-old son—who had his father's eyes, and was tall and handsome in his white dress shirt and dark slacks—take the new cadet oath with his classmates at the United States Military Academy at West Point.

* * * * *

*An Eaton
too hot to deny…*

National
bestselling author
**ROCHELLE
ALERS**

*Sweet
Southern
Nights*

Dr. Levi Eaton is worlds away from home. Still, the South has plenty of attractions—like the sexy and charming Angela Chase. But Angela's faith in men was destroyed by her fiancé's betrayal—and without the courage to trust, their sultry Southern nights may soon be just a haunting memory.…

"The story is beautifully crafted."
—*RT Book Reviews* on *BECAUSE OF YOU*

The Eatons

*Available the first week of March 2012
wherever books are sold.*

www.kimanipress.com

KPRA2480312

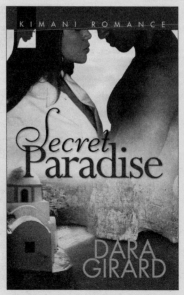

REQUEST YOUR FREE BOOKS!

2 FREE NOVELS
PLUS 2 FREE GIFTS!

KIMANI™
ROMANCE

Love's ultimate destination!

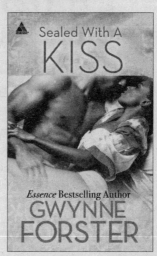